Voices

D0814644

Voices

An Open Door Book of Stories

Edited by Patricia Scanlan

NEW ISLAND

Voices: An Open Door Book of Stories
First published in 2020 by
New Island Books
Glenshesk House
10 Richview Office Park
Clonskeagh
Dublin 14, D14 V8C4
Republic of Ireland

www.newisland.ie

Individual contributions © Respective Authors, 2020
Foreword © Patricia Scanlan, 2020
'Gruyère in the Desmond' by Blindboy Boatclub is an adaptation of the
original story from *Boulevard Wren and Other Stories* (Gill Books, 2019).
'Cell 13' by Carlo Gébler has appeared in longer form in *The Wing
Orderly's Tales* (2016) published by New Island Books. 'Where it all
Began' by Úna-Minh Kavanagh is adapted from her memoir *Anseo*
(2019) published by New Island Books.

Print ISBN: 978-1-84840-782-4
eBook ISBN: 978-1-84840-788-6

Typeset by JVR Creative, India
Cover design by Mariel Deegan
Cover image from Shutterstock
Printed by ScandBook, scandbook.com

New Island Books is a member of Publishing Ireland.

10 9 8 7 6 5 4 3 2 1

'The journey of a lifetime starts with
the turning of a page.'

Rachel Anders

Also in the Open Door series:

And many more…

Contents

Foreword

Voices is a collection from some of Ireland's foremost writers. They have given their creative skills, time and energy to write a short story or piece of non-fiction to enhance the reading experience of emerging readers. *Voices* has been published to celebrate the 40th anniversary of the National Adult Literacy Agency (NALA).

NALA is a charity and membership-based organisation. It works to support adults with unmet literacy and numeracy needs so they can take part fully in society, and have access to learning opportunities that meet those needs. (See page 200 for more information on literacy supports.)

Before I became a full-time writer, I worked in Dublin Public Libraries. I often met people who had issues with reading and writing. They desperately wanted to improve their skills in both. I met literacy tutors who were frustrated at the lack of suitable material for the emerging reader.

My first novels were published in the early 90s. At that time, a literacy tutor jokingly said to me that I should write a novel for my local literacy group. It gave me food for thought. Could I write a book suitable for people who were improving their literacy skills? Could I write a story that would make the emerging reader want to turn the page?

I did write that book, and it was called *Second Chance*. I spent a long time writing it. In some ways I felt it was the most important book of my career, a true test of an author. At first it was difficult. I was mindful of keeping the sentences short and the language accessible. I wanted the reader to be engaged, eager to turn the page. I was nervous giving the manuscript to the literacy tutor and NALA.

Second Chance was published in 1994. Feedback from literacy groups was extremely positive. I was invited to speak to emerging readers, countrywide. I presented literacy certificates to students. Their courage and determination humbled me. It was inspiring to see people reach their goal and become empowered.

I approached New Island in 1998. My aim was to publish a series of literacy novellas written by well-known Irish writers. Edwin Higel, the publisher, and Ciara Considine, the commissioning editor, were enthusiastic about the idea. Open Door was born. We were determined that the books would have the highest production values. We had an immensely gratifying response from the authors we approached to take part in the project. Many of these novellas are original works and are enjoyed by readers of all ages.

At the moment, we are discussing our ninth series. We have now published fifty-four books. These include novellas, a poetry book and eight Irish language translations. We have sold thousands of copies and the rights have been sold abroad. The concept is very simple and effective and has far surpassed our original vision for the series. Open Door is not only for emerging readers with literacy difficulties. It has now become an educational aid to those interested in improving their English language and reading skills. Many immigrant groups here in Ireland are now using the books to help students improve their English. They are also used for the same purpose in the UK. Many teachers are using them in secondary schools to encourage teenage readers to get into the habit of reading. The goal is to promote the joy of reading so that the students will go on to read full-length novels.

The pieces in *Voices* are fascinating, thought-provoking and evocative. They are written by highly acclaimed, bestselling authors, who sell millions of books worldwide.

It is a privilege and honour, as the editor of this inspiring book, to introduce these fine writers to a new audience. Even though they are all busy with projects of their own, they have been so generous. They have gladly shared their creativity and time to contribute, and crafted their writing to suit our guidelines. There aren't enough words to thank them. They are all very special people who have touched the lives of many. Open Door, and this book, would not exist without them.

A big thanks also to my inspiring colleagues Edwin Higel, Mariel Deegan, Stephen Reid, Caoimhe Fox and all the team at New Island for their stellar work on *Voices*, and their ongoing commitment to Open Door. Huge thanks also to Helen Ryan Policy Officer National Adult Literacy Agency (NALA) for her expert advice and edits.

Big thanks also to the Department of Rural and Community Development, and Libraries Ireland, for providing funding to buy these books for library services throughout Ireland.

Thanks also to The Reading Agency UK for their ongoing support and encouragement through the years, since Open Door began in 1998.

We are extremely grateful to An Post for their generous support.

Finally, and most importantly, dear reader, our collective wish for you, is that *Voices*, empowers you, as you continue on your journey with reading. We hope *Voices* enhances your reading experience in every way. May it bring as much joy and delight to you, as it has to all of us who have been involved in creating it.

Warmest wishes,

Patricia Scanlan
Series Editor

Patricia Scanlan.

Gruyère in the Desmond
Blindboy Boatclub

'The Greeks would want a word with themselves now with their hard cheeses.' That was the Chin's reaction to the halloumi, having previously tasted the feta. To which he asserted, 'I don't need to be hearing my food squeak inside in my head like a rat.'

The Desmond Arms was a grand pub. Nothing fancy – not manky either, though. It was grand. Bang of lemon cleaner off the jacks floor seats. It would normally be a quiet pub, too, until we would take out the cheese in front of the Chin on Tuesdays. Guppy would travel from Tesco with a selection, and there would be a blindfold for the Chin, made out of a tea-towel. And then Guppy would impale the little piece of cheese on a cocktail stick and hover it in front of the Chin's open mouth. You would see little flickers of terror in his body, jiggling the fat belly,

15

jolts, fear of the surprise of something new. The whole pub beyond our group, even the real old lads, would have their heads in their pints, but in the way that they would have one ear towards the Chin. Waiting, like it's a penalty shoot-out, to hear the reactions out of him. He would take the cheese on the tongue and surrender it in, crumbs around the lips and all. And you would watch his face dragging and pulling. Head on him like a terrier with a ball. A groan would be let out. I don't think there was ever a cheese he liked. And when the groan surfaced, we would all howl – the whole place would scream laughing. Bellies all over the place.

Guppy would say, 'Out of ten, Chin, what is she out of ten?' and the Chin would say, 'She is a four. What did you call her again?' 'Gruyère,' Guppy would say. 'Gree-yair.' The Chin would purse the lips again, and you would know the pokey tongue was searching around the gob to assess the situation. 'She is like a Kerry-man's dustbin.' And the pub would shake from men's laughter. Guppy would go up to the dartboard and write on the slate: 'Gruyère 4/10, Kerry-man's dustbin'. The blindfold would come off the Chin, and he would be clean into a Carr's cracker and his IPA to wash down the cheese.

Gruyère was the last cheese the Chin tasted before they found him hanging against the door of his upstairs bedroom. He had taped off the bottom of the stairs with a full roll and stuck a little cardboard sign on the tape barrier that said, 'Do not come up the stairs, just phone the guards. I am sorry', so as his daughter Ciara would not have to see his body.

Stilton, Gouda, provolone, Munster, Cheddar, pecorino, Camembert, mozzarella, Havarti, ricotta, Edam, Manchego, Roquefort, Emmental. You might as well have been carving those names into gravestones up in Mount Saint Kenneth.

We started the group in 2015. There were sixteen of us. By 2019, that was down to eleven. Jarlath Purcell, 53; Ger 'Rusty' Riordan, 48; Caleb 'Elbows' Wallis, 52; Finbar Kinsella, 49; and Bernard 'the Chin' Collopy, 50. All dead men.

The Brothers of Gatch was a weekly meet-up of some old pals from school. A gatch is a way of walking, a stride on you, like an 'I am not here to start hassle but I will finish it' kind of a gatch. The group began with myself and Guppy in The Desmond Arms, 24 March 2015, for two reasons.

The first reason was the situation with the taps. The Desmond, I knew, for thirty-odd years, had only ever four taps: Guinness, Harp, Budweiser and Bulmers.

But then they brought in the craft beers to draw a few students – at first in bottles and then on tap. The students never came. But men get curious. And you would have a Saltwater IPA or a Saison or an Oyster Stout – studied sips, then hungry gulps, before realising you had been missing out all along. And four taps turned to twelve, and two taps would have a guest beer each month.

The second reason we started the Brothers of Gatch was the new selection of cheeses below in Lidl and Tesco. Mad quare beige lumps with names that sounded like they fell off buses. One night, myself and Guppy were drinking a pair of sour grapefruit ales, and he said, 'Sure, this is like wine. We might as well have cheese too.' So we did. I strolled over beyond to the Tesco across on Mallow Street and plucked a few odd cheeses out of the fridge. Brought them in the door of the Desmond, placed them on beer mats and we ate them with fingers on us. Started ordering different beers out of the taps too, and tasting them with new cheeses, mix-and-match, like, and it was powerful. It brought something to the pub, to myself and Guppy's friendship. I do not know what it was, but it was not just pints anymore. It was not dark.

When the cheese and the craft beers were brought in, it felt like a game, and you would be

18

excited for it every Tuesday evening. So we invited more men in, fine men – clerks, joiners, engineers, men we knew a long time – and we would all have a new craft beer and a new cheese each week, and we would talk about it, hop ball, write reviews on the dartboard, and it was like being back in sixth year of St Clement's again.

There was a third reason we started the group. We never spoke about the third reason. Even though the third reason is more powerful than the first and second reasons.

There is a blackness that comes over men. It's a dark fright. And you cannot look straight at it, and you cannot say out loud that it's there. But you know it when you feel it first thing in the morning and you just cannot figure out what the point of being alive is. The thought of that brings this sharp dread and after that, I suppose, an olive sadness – no, a green loneliness, a feeling of being trapped purely by just being awake or alive. And it will slowly take away all the things you would normally enjoy, like a film, or a match, or a song. And it will slice bits off of you until you need a pint to clean the wound. And not even the pints would sort it, they only numb it. That was the third reason we started the Brothers of Gatch. In from the hovering grey cold of Tuesday nights.

The third reason would only be noted over Emmental or a cloudy cider, through purple skin under eyes and red noses. Little yellow glances at each other. Never words. Just gestures. Through slags and pats on backs and digs in shoulders. I knew. He knew. They knew. This was never about cheese or craft beer. It was an unspoken contract. Turning our faces away from the forever pull of the solitude. It was an agreement. We all suffered under the same loneliness. Not the loneliness of being alone, it was not that – sure, we all had our families and wives – but the mystery emptiness of feeling alone when you are anything but.

On nights with pints I would stare up at a bottle of Cutty Sark above the bar – the yellow and black label with the ship would draw me in. It had about twenty sails, and I would think of myself at the helm, and all around are little islands, and I'm searching them for the man I used to be. He is lost, but in the heart of me, I know he is gone. And I sail on the big mad nothing sea that screams wind in my face. I investigate from island to island. I find feck all. I still wander into the dead bony forests and shale rocks. And one day, I will go so deep into one of the islands that I cannot see back to the ship. On

20

that day, I'll lie down against a tree and let death have me. That is a balls of a way to be.

And if I ever got that look on me, staring up at the Cutty Sark, one of the lads would draw me back and ask me what I thought of the Stilton. They were like a lighthouse. Just something glimmering off in the distance for me to reach towards. Something different than the empty islands.

Lüneberg, Nut Brown, Herve, Red Ale, Danish Blue, Weiss, Clonakilty Swiss, Blond. In the map in my head, the islands became a cheese or a beer with each expedition.

We began to notice our own little dark rituals – the moment that your head would leave the pub and you would entertain the dread. The thousand-yard stare, I suppose, but we had never been to war. For me it was the bottle of Cutty Sark. After Caleb Wallis was found below in the river, God rest him, Guppy went back on the John Player. If he went outside and took too long, you would see him standing and gazing, the fag long with ash down to the butt. Him drifting in towards the empty. I would want to ask him what he saw when he stared, but you could never ask that. And you would shout, 'Come in before Jarlath eats all the Roquefort you eejit.' And we would laugh and he

21

would come back into the pub, and then you would have saved him.

For John Paul Noonan it was when he would start picking at the label off his beer, so you would get him a pint glass. Eddie would take his jacket on and off like he was leaving. Finucane might go to the jacks for a very long piss. Christy Walsh would touch his chest and ask what the symptoms of a heart attack were. Andy Fitz would get a blank stare and snap himself out by starting an argument with you. The Chin, the poor old Chin, would have pink eyes with tears over them, and that is when we would give him a blindfold and give him laughter. These were little devices, unique to each of us, that would let the others know that you were staring at the emptiness. And we would all know this, but we would never say it, and we would save each other every Tuesday night.

'Go for a run,' my doctor would say to me. 'Have you tried meditating?' 'This happens to men of your age. I will book you in for a prostate check.'

The Brothers of Gatch knew what was wrong without words or diagnoses.

That Special Moment

Dermot Bolger

This childhood memory is so slight that I ask myself why I recall it so well. I think it is because it was the moment when I sensed that, one day I would become a writer. However I was too young back then to understand what I was feeling.

But I remember the day so clearly. I can still smell the floor polish on the shining lino. I still feel the grains of sand stuck between my bare toes when I crossed the big bedroom. I still feel warm summer air coming in the open window. I am upstairs in Mrs Butler's guesthouse, a mile outside Courtown in Wexford. It is my family's summer holiday in 1969. Flies swarm under trees near the house. Crickets chirp from the long grass. Aged ten, I sit alone on one of three beds in a large back room. Here at night, my parents sleep in one bed and my sister in another. My older brother and I share the third bed.

My father is a sailor. He only enjoys nights at home with his family in Finglas if his ship is loading in Dublin Port. This is what makes summer holidays so special. We are all together. The summer of 1969 is not our first holiday in Mrs Butler's. But it will be our last. Some months later – days before Christmas – my mother dies. Childhood changes for me forever. But, as a child sitting alone upstairs in that guesthouse, there is no hint of sorrow to come. Mrs Butler's house feels huge. The steps to her kitchen are out of bounds. Other families also stay there. A Cork family seem posh because they have a car parked on the gravel. The boy whose father owns this car dances to a song, 'Viva Bobby Joe', playing on the radio.

At night other music fills the night air in Courtown. At dusk in the swirling lights of a fairground, a song by The Seekers blares from loudspeakers. It is called 'The Carnival Is Over'. For years after I cannot listen to it. It brings back too many memories. The funfair smells of chips and hot dogs. Children run in the shadows, faces covered in candyfloss. I walk among booths where men try to win prizes. Teenage girls whirl overhead, screaming in the swing-chairs that spin around.

Mrs Butler is kindly but I am slightly scared of her. Mary – her gentle, elderly helper – carries jugs of milk from a nearby farm. The boy from Cork goes to play pitch and putt with his father. I tag along excitedly. On the first tee his father asks me if I wish to hit one shot. Golf is new to me. I raise the club, nervous and excited. A man comes running. He shouts that I have not paid. My club stops inches from the ball. I am afraid to hit it. The Cork father does not offer to pay for me. My fingers long to have struck a golf ball just once.

Beside Mrs Butler's house is a field with a pond. I play alone there. Loud crickets sing everywhere. I cannot spy them, despite spending hours searching. A donkey watches me with patient eyes. Flies buzz around his face. My brother and the Cork boy kick ball on the gravel. Local children stand at Mrs Butler's gate to watch them, like they are film stars. My mother comes to the front door. She calls us in for dinner. There are desserts I am afraid to taste. They look like the frog-spawn in the pond. The adults at the table talk about gangs of Hells Angels seen in nearby seaside towns. A mile away in the dusk, Courtown throbs with the sins I have yet to discover.

After my mother dies there are no more family holidays. A quarter century passes before I visit

Courtown again. By then I am a father myself. Driving my young sons to a hotel in Rosslare, I decide to show them Mrs Butler's. As a child I was here so often that I should be able to find it. But I spend an hour circling small roads. I pass her house three times before I realise that I am back again, as an adult, outside it.

Standing at the rusting padlocked gate, I need to ask the man next door if this is the right house. It looks so tiny, closed down and empty. Mrs Butler is long dead. I cannot believe that this is the same garden where I played. The room where we ate our meals looks so small. I look down the road. In my mind's eye, I can see the stooped figure of Mary carrying milk. I can see my family leave this house, setting off for another day on Courtown beach. I remember us waiting for that magic moment of catching our first glimpse of the sea. I can see us walking home from the funfair at night.

The road is so small that my car blocks it. I do not climb the wall to peer into the empty rooms. Instead I close my eyes. In my mind I walk again up those stairs, with the long week stretching ahead. I remember that moment when my family went downstairs and left me alone. Later I will understand the feelings that came over me as I sat there. I will recognise it as the moment when poems entered my head. But at ten years old I was just puzzled by this feeling of wanting to stop time, to remember everything about that moment. The summer air blowing through the window. The drone of crickets. The sand between my toes. I remember sitting there, tired and happy. I remember pressing my forehead against the window. I know I will never forget that room. Then I hear my brother call me from the stairs. I turn and run happily down to my family. None of us know what joys and sorrows are to come.

A Good Woman
Marita Conlon-McKenna

I did not even get to say goodbye to her. I was not given the chance to hold her hand, hug her or even say a word to her. It was unbearable. My older sister, Linda, had been the only one in the family let see Mam in the hospital. And then for only twenty minutes, while having to wear a mask and protective clothing.

Mam must have been terrified, surrounded by nurses and doctors dressed like space men. Linda had filmed her on her phone, but it upset me to watch it. Mam was like a pale white bird, fighting to breathe, barely able to open her eyes.

* * *

She had worked nearly all her life and reared five of us. Made sure everything ran smoothly. There was food on the table, clean clothes and fresh made beds. She and Da had been a great pair. They took us up the Dublin Mountains for drives and walks on a Sunday. Once the good weather came in, there were picnics on the beaches in Dollymount Strand and Bray.

She and Da went to Doyle's pub twice a month with their friends. Once a month, on Sunday evening, she dressed up and they both went dancing.

Her dancing days had ended when Da died. We had worried about her being lonely but she had just got on with it. She helped with the local Meals on Wheels, delivering food to the elderly in her old Fiesta. Every Tuesday morning she helped to clean the church. On Thursday she minded Linda's youngest lad after school.

Mam always had green fingers. She had turned Da's potato and vegetable patch into beautiful flowerbeds. His old work shed was now her potting shed.

She went on holidays with her two best friends, Sheila and Angela, both widows like herself. Still, I always made sure that Mam joined me, Jen and the kids for at least a week of the summer, in our mobile home down in Wexford.

Four years ago, she had to get a new hip. Mam had been nervous about it all. A few days before the operation she had made a will splitting everything equally between the five of us. Then she had made a list of exactly what she wanted for her funeral.

'Mam, we'll have no sad talk like that,' Linda had bossed after buying a load of new nightdresses for her hospital stay.

The new hip had worked a treat. After only a few weeks on crutches, Mam was back to her usual self.

* * *

She had been painting the shed when she fell. Bill Casey from next door heard her cry for help. He went in and phoned the ambulance. No one was going near the hospitals, as there was an outbreak of a strange virus. There was even talk of a total lockdown of the country.

'Strictly no visitors' we were told, because of Covid.

So, Mam went in the ambulance alone. Her head was stitched and she had to have an operation to fix her ankle. We phoned her every day.

The schools were closed and then my work had shut. Everyone had to work or study from home. You were only let go to the grocery shop or the chemist or for a short walk.

Jen said the kids were driving her bonkers, always under her feet. Paddy was studying for his exams. Young Karl spent all day on the PlayStation. Anna, our daughter, was upset as she couldn't even visit us with her new baby.

The doctor phoned to tell us that Mam had got worse. Real sick.

Covid! She had tested positive for the virus.

Linda was the only one let in to see her. The nurse told her not to touch, kiss or hug Mam. It was cruel.

Mam's instructions for her funeral were written out. There was a list of her favourite readings and songs for the church. She had named who was to do everything. She wanted her funeral lunch to be held in Doyle's pub, for old times' sake.

'Ten people only at funerals,' John Hegarty, the undertaker had told us. 'I'm sorry but it's the law.'

Ten people! How could we have just ten people at the funeral? Mam had five kids, all married. Seventeen grandchildren and two great grandchildren. Then there were my aunts and uncles, her best friends, and the neighbours.

There would be no church service, and we had to go straight to the grave.

Father Frank was sorry but he would not even be able to say the prayers over the coffin at the graveyard. Like many priests of his age he had to cocoon. Father Albert, the new priest from Africa, would do it instead.

There had been right old family arguments trying to pick out ten of us to attend the funeral. A deep anger grew in me at how Mam's life was ending. Surely she deserved better than this? Karl said that some bats in China had bitten a pangolin, which had caused the virus. Jen read that it came from an accident in a laboratory.

Now half the world was getting sick. There was not a plane in the sky or hardly a car on the road. Poor Mam could not even have the decency of a proper funeral Mass because some fool fancied eating a bit of pangolin!

* * *

The sun was shining bright the morning of her funeral. We had told the driver of the hearse to drive past Mam's house on the way to the graveyard, to pass the place where we had all grown up.

We drove slowly and the minute we turned into the street, all the neighbours were out, keeping their distance. Jen and the rest of family were there. And all the grandchildren with cards and flowers were there too. They clapped and waved as Mam passed.

Dave was blubbing like a kid and Linda held his hand so tight her nails dug into his skin. Claire and Conor both recorded the funeral on their phones. There was a crowd outside Doyle's too. Old Father Frank and all Mam's friends from the parish were standing outside Saint Teresa's waving them on.

At the graveyard it hit me hard. I watched as they lowered Mam's coffin down into the grave to finally join Da.

Father Albert led us in the prayers. Sheila and Angela made us sing three of Mam's favourite hymns, and our voices carried over the quiet of the graveyard.

'Your mother was a good woman.' Father Albert smiled. 'She had a big heart. She invited me to tea with her a few times. She showed me how to cook rashers and sausages and how to make her special shepherd's pie. I will always think of her kindness to me. '

Afterwards we ate sandwiches and had mugs of tea and a few beers, sitting outside in our coats, in

Linda's back garden. The birds were singing as we laughed and recalled all the good times with her.

Mam was like Father Albert said, a good woman, a good neighbour and friend, a good sister, mother, grandmother and great-grandmother. She had filled our lives and the lives of all those around her with love and kindness. Covid or not, big funeral or not, Mam with her big heart was a woman who would always be remembered.

Rock Star
Sinéad Crowley

'Ladies and gentlemen, back in their hometown for one night only, I give you – LUNCH BREAK!'

Chris strides on to the stage, grabs the mike and starts to sing. Everyone is on their feet, clapping and cheering. It has been more than twenty years since I first saw the band perform. It looks like little has changed. Out in the audience I can see Tina, dancing with her family and friends. Still blonde, still tiny. Rocking a black top and skinny jeans, she could pass for seventeen. The first song ends and Chris holds up his hand for silence.

'This one is called, "I Take Your Hand".'

There is another huge cheer. Chris closes his eyes, holding the mike close for a moment before starting to sing.

'You do not think I see you but I do. You are not some little girl …'

He stays like that for a moment. The first notes of the chorus ring out. He opens his eyes and begins to pace up and down the stage. Every woman in the room is wishing the song had been written for her. I close my eyes and remember the night I thought it had been.

We did everything together, Tina and I, when we were seventeen. We went to school together. We hung out together at weekends. We drove our parents up the wall as we stayed out longer, later and further away. We were able to get into clubs in town by then too. So when she told me one Saturday that we were going to a concert at a nearby boys' school, I thought she was joking. But no, it turned out some of the local lads were in a band. She fancied the lead singer. That was the night we met Chris. That was the night that everything changed.

The band was called Lunch Break. It was supposed to be a joke name. But as soon as Chris walked onto the tiny school stage I could see that music was not a joke to him. The rest of them were pretty awful. Only the drummer came close to matching him for talent. When Chris sang, I forgot there was anyone else in the room.

We all went to the pub together afterwards. After downing a couple of vodkas for Dutch courage, I sat down next to him.

'Hi. Well done. I thought you were brilliant.'

'Do you think so?' Chris began. 'That's really nice—'

And then Tina bounded over, blonde hair bouncing. She was carrying a tray of pints. As she pushed in beside us and offered Chris a cigarette, I wondered why I had even bothered to try. When they kissed at the end of the night, nobody was surprised. When Tina asked me if I would be ok going home on my own, I told her it was no problem. The young drummer overheard and offered to walk with me. He was a nice enough fella. When we got to my front gate he wrote his phone number on a used bus ticket. I took it, just to be polite. But Chris was the only musician on my mind.

My nieces do not believe me when I tell them what it was like back then, with no YouTube and no streaming. If you wanted to make it in the music business, you had to play a lot of gigs and hope people would start talking about you. And someone did notice Lunch Break, six months after that first concert. Colin, the drummer, rang me. We were good mates at that stage. He told me that some people from a record company were coming over to see them play a support set in the Baggot Inn.

We all went to a party in Chris's house that night. Tina and the rest of the lads were in great form. They were knocking back cans and talking about how they were going to be on *Top of the Pops* within the year. But Chris and Colin were much quieter. They knew this was their big chance.

Chris and Tina had a fight and she stormed off but he didn't go after her. Instead he took out his guitar and began to play a brand new song. I thought it was beautiful and, because it was dark, and no one could see me blushing, I began to sing along. Chris had never heard me sing before, no one had. But that night, I sang for him. The song was called 'I Take Your Hand' and after we had finished, Chris joked that he should give me a co-writing credit. Lunch Break played the Baggot Inn a week later and the men from London loved them. They weren't on *Top of the Pops* a year later. It only took them six months. 'I Take Your Hand' went to number one. Chris never did give me that credit.

A roar from the crowd brings me back to the present. I blink and smile as Chris gives a final wave then walks off stage.

'That was amazing.'

Then he reaches down and gives me a massive hug.

'I mean it, Natalie. I thought I would never be up on a stage again. I owe you one.'

'No problem.'

I smile as he leaves and then take a deep breath. I usually like to spend time on my own before a concert but this isn't a big gig. It is just a fundraiser for the hospital in my home town. I agreed to do it as soon as they asked me, but I had just one request – that Lunch Break be asked to open the show. It was Tina's idea actually. We're still friends and when she told me she wanted to do something special for Chris's fortieth birthday, we came up with this plan. The girl who was promoting the concert hadn't heard of Lunch Break. She was only a baby when they had their one and only hit single back in 1992. But when you've sold as many records as I have, people tend to say yes when you ask them things.

'Ready?'

Colin walks up and squeezes my arm. When Lunch Break broke up, he and Chris came back to Dublin, Chris to marry Tina and join his Dad's business and Colin, well, he came back to me. And it turned out we were perfect partners in more ways than one. We started writing songs together, and then performing them. He'd learned so much with Lunch Break that we didn't get fooled by the music business second time around. This year we even brought the kids on tour.

'Ready!'

I smile at my husband and walk forward onto the stage.

The Devil You Know
Martina Devlin

In the beginning, I disliked Adam. Not that anybody cared how I felt. Adam and God treated me like a doll. I was intended to be his plaything. Nothing more.

God made me from Adam's rib and handed me over to him. He did everything except wrap me in tissue paper and tie a bow around my middle. Any woman would be provoked.

So there is Adam, stretched out in a meadow making daisy chains, when up pops God with me tucked under his arm.

'Here you go, Adam. A little something to amuse you.'

'Thanks, God. You shouldn't have.'

'Don't mention it. Just something I threw together in my free time. Toss it away if it does not please you. I can try my hand at another model.'

'No, I like the look of this one. But what should I do with it? Snack on it? Scrub my back with it?'

'It is your companion. I thought you might be lonely when I am busy in my workshop, tweaking creation.'

'Now that you mention it, God, sometimes I do feel a bit empty. You are the best. You think of everything. What does a companion do, exactly?'

'Whatever you want it to. You are the boss. I call it a woman. Quite pleased with my handiwork, to tell you the truth. Now we have the full set. Man and woman. One of each.'

'Woman. Hello, woman. You belong to me.'

Standing there in paradise, my blood began to boil at the way they chattered about me as though I was invisible. Neither of them considered my feelings.

'It is nicer if she has her own name,' said God. 'Helps with bonding.'

'Oh, I see. How about Adamette? Or Adamina?'

'Bit of a mouthful. Let us give her a snappier name. Eve has a certain ring to it. Here you go. Enjoy her. Oh, by the way, the same rule about avoiding the Tree of Knowledge applies to Eve. It is a no-go zone. I'll leave you to explain it. Bye for now.'

'Wait, God, I am not sure I like the name Eve. Can I call her something else?'

'Afraid I've already registered her with Gabriel as Eve. He spied us on the way over and nabbed me on the spot. A stickler for recordkeeping, our Gabriel. You will get used to Eve. It does not take long to say. That is always a plus.'

Just as he was turning away, God noticed I had turned red. He thought I was embarrassed because I was naked. It never occurred to him that I was fuming. Anyhow, feeling sorry for me, he touched the crown of my head with his forefinger. I felt a tingle, followed by a swelling. All at once my hair rippled down my back and past my knees. It kept going until it reached my feet. God was giving me something to wrap around my skin, if being bare troubled me.

Which it never did. Why should it? I was the original woman. All beauty standards sprang from me. Even Adam – never the sharpest member of the human race, except when he was the only one – recognised that. As soon as we were alone, he walked around and around, admiring me.

'Me Adam. You Eve.'

Naturally I ignored him. Rude individual. Not so much as a 'how do you do?' or 'I believe we are related through our bone structure.'

He thought I did not understand when I refused to answer him.

'I suppose I will have to teach you to talk,' he said. 'I was created knowing how to use language.

43

I expect you will need lessons. We will do two hours every morning.'

I had a secret self he was unaware of. I could speak just as well as him, if not better. But I preferred to let Adam think he was shaping and improving me, if it pleased him – as it did.

And so our life in paradise developed a pattern. Adam bossing me about and me resisting being bossed, unless it suited me. He was happy with his God-given companion. But, between you and me, there were times when I was irritated by the arrangement.

Often, God dropped in for a visit but old Beardy never paid much attention to me. I saw through him. It made him uneasy. It was clear he only wanted to boast about something new he had invented in that junkshop of his. You should have seen him strut the day he created the rainbow.

Whenever God and Adam settled down for a natter, I would slip away. There was only so much I could swallow of:

'So, I took the hyena and added a laugh, just for jollies.'

'God, you are brilliant. I do not know where you get your ideas from.'

One day, I met an amazing creature. Looking back, I suppose he was lying in wait for me. My new friend was sleek, eye-catching, charming and interested in me. He asked about things. Nobody else did that. With legs, he would have been perfect.

He led me to the Tree of Knowledge. Tongue flicking with excitement he described the flavour of its fruit. It tasted of birthdays, sunshine and birdsong. But that was nothing compared to its effect. One bite and you understood everything. All secrets were revealed. All mysteries explained.

I never hesitated. I reached out, plucked an apple and bit it.

There was nothing special about the taste. But once I had started I kept going. Right down to the core.

Adam found me as I was chewing the last mouthful. My new friend vanished as soon as he saw him. But Adam only had eyes for the apple stalk I was holding.

'You did not eat it,' he cried.

'I did. And you should too.'

'God would hate it.'

That was good enough for me. I picked an apple and handed it to him. He hummed and hawed, wondering if he should risk a nibble or not. In the end, he tasted a morsel.

The next thing we know, Beardy shows up looking stern and disappointed. And the pair of us are marched out of paradise by a band of sour-faced angels.

It was the best thing that ever happened to Adam and me. Not that he saw it the same way. In fact, he was never particularly grateful. But I would do it again. Not because I learned anything worthwhile from tasting the apple. I didn't. But because it changed things.

We had to work for a living rather than wander about admiring moon beams. We had to work as a team, use our wits, and perfect the art of survival. Adam lived in hope that God would pardon him. He wore his knees out, praying for it. As for me, I managed without forgiveness. Paradise is overrated. I never really warmed to the place.

Out in the world, we felt pain, hunger and fear. But there were compensations. I suppose you could say Adam lost paradise and gained a wife. Yes, I learned to value his loyalty and affection, and became a willing mate to him. Mostly.

That forbidden fruit business taught me something, you see. Better the devil you know.

All Around the World
Roddy Doyle

The house was small and it was full. The whole family had come home for the Coronavirus. There was Ryan and his ma, his three big sisters and four small nephews. And his granny.

They were all stuck in the house and it was mad. His granny sat in the kitchen in her wheelchair. They all had to go around her.

'Is the lock up over yet?' she asked.

'It's the lockdown, Granny,' said Ryan.

'Yes,' she said. 'But is it over?'

'No,' said Ryan.

He felt bad when he said that.

'Not yet,' he said.

'I want to go for a walk,' said his granny.

'You can't,' he said. 'You have to stay inside. To keep you safe.'

He had walked around the wheelchair six times by the time he said this.

'I feel like I am only twenty-one,' said his granny. 'I want to go to London and New York.'

His granny had been to Belfast. Once. That was as far as she had ever gone.

Ryan was feeling dizzy. He was still walking around the wheelchair.

The schools were shut, so the four boys were doing their school lessons at the kitchen table. Well, one of them was at the table. Two of them were on top of the table. And the last one was climbing into the fridge. The teacher that day was one of Ryan's sisters. But she was upstairs having her hair done by his other two sisters. His ma was hiding in the attic.

Ryan had an idea.

'I'll bring you to London,' he said.

He opened the back door and pushed the wheelchair down the ramp, into the garden. The garden was as big as a bed and it wasn't a double bed.

'Welcome to London, Granny,' said Ryan. 'What do you want to see?'

His granny laughed.

'Ah, brilliant,' she said. 'I want to see the big clock. What's it called? Big Bill.'

'Big Ben,' said Ryan.

'That's the one,' said his granny.

Ryan pushed the chair around the garden. He pointed at the back wall.

'There is Big Ben,' he said.

'I forgot my glasses,' said his granny. 'Is Big Ben big?'

'Big Ben is massive,' said Ryan.

They laughed again.

Ryan pointed.

'And look at even Bigger Ben beside him,' he said.

Half an hour later, they went back up the ramp and into the kitchen and the madness.

'Home sweet home,' said his granny.

The next morning when Ryan went into the kitchen, his granny had her coat on.

'We'll go to Paris today,' she said.

Ryan opened the back door.

'Please have your passports ready,' he said.

They went down the ramp, into the garden.

'Are we there yet?' Ryan's granny asked.

'We are,' said Ryan. 'What do you want to see?'

'I want to see the tower,' she said. 'What is it called? The Blackpool Tower.'

'The Eiffel Tower,' said Ryan.

'That's the one,' said his granny.

Ryan pushed the chair around the garden. He stopped. He pointed at the trampoline in the garden next door.

'There it is,' he said.

'We'll go up to the top,' said his granny.

'Ah, here,' he said. 'I'll have to carry you.'

He grunted as he pushed his granny around the garden. Once. Twice. Three times.

'You've been eating too much pasta, granny,' he said.

She guffawed.

'It is the chair,' she said. 'The chair has been sucking up the spaghetti.'

It started to rain.

'We had better go home,' said Ryan's granny.

'I know a shortcut,' said Ryan.

They were up the ramp and into the house in three seconds flat. It was a normal school day in the kitchen. The four boys were up on the table. They were doing the 1916 Rising.

'Who's winning?' Ryan's granny asked.

'Batman,' said Ryan's sister, Holly.

'Is Batman Irish?' Ryan's granny asked.

'He is this morning,' said Holly. 'The poor Brits haven't a hope.'

The next morning, Ryan's granny was waiting for

Ryan.

'Where are we going today?' Ryan asked.

'I'd like to see New York,' said his granny.

They went down the ramp, into the garden.

'That took forever,' said Ryan's granny.

'What do you want to see?' Ryan asked.

'The statue,' said his granny. 'What is it called? The big girl in the water.'

'Liberty,' said Ryan.

'That's the one,' said his granny. 'We all need a bit of liberty. Let's go have a look at her.'

So. Every morning for more than two months, Ryan and his granny went to a different part of the world. Then they went back up the ramp for their breakfast.

One day, they heard it on the radio. Old people could leave the house. They could go outside. For a few hours. They heard the woman on the radio say it.

'Is she talking about me?' Ryan's granny asked.

'She is,' said Ryan.

The next morning they met in the kitchen.

'Where do you want to go today?' Ryan asked.

'I want to see Dublin,' said his granny.

Ryan turned the wheelchair and they went out the front door, and down a different ramp. They went down the path, out on to their street. They

51

went to the end of the street. They saw the Spire in the distance.

'What do you think of Dublin, Granny?' Ryan asked.

'I think I prefer Paris,' she said.

She laughed.

'Do you want to go home?' Ryan asked.

'I am home,' she said.

A gang of kids ran past. A bunch of boys on bikes flew past.

'This is home,' she said. 'I have always loved Dublin.'

A dog started to bark at them.

'Even the dogs are better in Dublin,' she said.

She turned her head as Ryan pushed the chair. She put her hand on Ryan's hand.

'Thank you for bringing me all over the world,' she said.

'You are welcome,' he said.

'But it is great to be home,' she said.

'Will we keep going?' he asked.

'We will,' she said. 'I don't care where we go.'

She patted his hand.

'As long as I am with you, love,' she said. 'That is all that matters.'

After the Fourth War

Christine Dwyer Hickey

On the landing stage at Chapo we waited for the early water bus. It was dark still and people sat on benches or stood by the walls. Not a word out of anyone.

I put my tired head against my grandmother's arm and looked out at the black river. I was twelve years old then, pretending to be nine. And I was dressed as a boy, a cousin I had never met. He lived with my grandmother for a few years before he died of the Spring Virus.

I had been with my grandmother for a week by then, and found her house, with its many rooms, grim and lonely. The road where she lived was full of dark and often empty houses. The gardens wild and made out of shadows. Like a place you might come across in a dream.

This was just after the end of the Fourth War and my first time to go into the city.

I was not of the city but one of the Mall people. I found the city people odd and shifty, the way they never looked you in the eye. My grandmother said that was because the small screens had all been taken away. They were learning how to look each other in the face again.

* * *

My grandmother had studied my face against the face of the dead boy on the red identity card. She held the mane of my hair in one hand. Her other hand cut and chopped behind me. It sounded like some small animal was trying to eat its way into my head.

She said, 'They won't let you next or near the clinic. But there's a doctor in a place called East Wall we can try. Do you people have doctors at all?'

She wanted to know everything about our lives in the Mall. She always called us 'you people'. But I didn't know how to explain our lives to her. How to say our ceilings are high and made out of glass. You can see the black sky at night, sometimes the stars. You can hear the rain as you go to sleep. There is

54

always the sound of voices. We have our own ways, our own diseases. When we die, we die. Then we are buried behind the old yellow car park.

* * *

On the outside, my grandmother was always calm: a sturdy shape, a wide black face, a bland and cat-like eye. She schooled me in her night-time kitchen. And woke me early and schooled me all over again.

'You are a boy now. That's the main thing. You are a boy and you feel well. If they find out that you're sick – that's it. It is all over. And do not say a word – ok? Even if you hear me tell a lie.'

'I know, you told me.'

'Good girl, I mean, good boy.'

* * *

On the morning we went for the water bus, she asked me about my mother. It was dark and cold as we went down her road but all I felt was the heat. My grandmother wore a heavy coat and a red fluffy hat. I wore the dead boy's clothes.

'And how is she anyway – your mother?'

'A bit lonely I think.'

'Pity she didn't think of that before she ran off with that … that. Not a word all this time and *now*? Lonely – ha! Lonely indeed.'

At the gate out of the estate, my grandmother pressed a bell. An old cop popped up in the hut and sleepy-eyed, slid the hatch open. She opened the top of a brown paper bag and out came the breath of warm buns. The cop shyly dipped his hand in. Then she asked him about his sore leg and said, 'Isn't it great now, to think that the war is over?'

He took out a yellow bun, 'Yes,' he said, 'until the next one comes along.'

The old cop grinned and then looked at me and said, 'Jaysus, isn't he after getting terrible tall?'

He pulled out a sheet of paper, then bang, bang, bang, stamped it all over. Then he gave it to my grandmother.

* * *

The cop on the landing stage was young. Outside on the bridge, two more of them walked up and down, two long guns slung on their backs. There were words on a wall that warned about false papers and permits. There was a picture of a man, his hands cuffed behind his back.

The cop took his time. I heard the stamp of his feet as he went up and down the line looking at papers. Behind him, the sound of lapping water and the creak, creak of big ropes. Now and then, he looked into a bag. Or he made someone stand up so he could search their pockets. An old man, on the far side of my grandmother, gave a loud tut.

A few places ahead of us, was a man who looked like Tarek – the man who took me to my grandmother's house. He must have been from Syria. A girl was with him. She was about my age – my real age. The girl stared at me as if she knew who I was.

When the cop came near, my grandmother gave me a nudge with her elbow. I stood up and went to the end of the jetty as if I only wanted to look out for the water bus. Across the way, I saw the twists of smoke from camp fires. Up river, the lamps of boats bobbed all over the inky water. I tried to work out where my home was from here. Down river anyway and to the west on the old motorway. I thought of all the other malls along the old M50 and the people who lived in them. As we did, on the outskirts of the city. 'Outskirts for outcasts', as my father used to say.

When I turned back to look at my grandmother, the cop was beside her. He was holding her cards like a fan in his hand.

My grandmother was speaking too fast, too loud. 'His mother is dead,' she said. 'His father killed in the war and yes, I am his grandmother. That's my permit there and that one is his card. And the pink one is for ...'

The cop looked at her, 'I know what they are,' he said.

From the far side of the landing stage, I could almost feel her fear in my hand.

The cop gave the papers and cards back to her, went into the office and closed the door. And then the old man beside my grandmother blew his nose.

I heard the grind and groan of the water bus. Then a blast of light and the sound of chains. Two men in yellow macs helped my grandmother along a ramp. I walked behind. Below deck, all the people from the landing stage began to sit down. And not a word out of any of them.

I had never been this close to water. I had never been on any sort of a boat before and so I asked to stay up on deck.

'Too cold,' she said.

'Not for me.'

She took off her glove and put her hand on my forehead.

'Five minutes to cool down and then back down here to me.'

The dark had gone out of the sky by now, leaving a soft dove-grey light over the river. The boat shoved through the water. Sometimes it stopped on the left bank. The next time, it crossed at a slant to the right side. At every stop, the big ropes were thrown to a man on the dock. The gate on the boat was pushed open and the men in yellow macs helped people on and off.

We passed under a bridge and the river spread out between high walls. Way above the walls, I saw the dome of a mosque on one side and the peak of a church on the other. Above that again, a tall glass tower with cops moving around inside it. I heard the sounds of the city over the walls, but not who or what these sounds belonged to.

When I came below deck again, something had changed. The old man was talking. And then another man and a woman. And now laughing. They were talking about the past, and I don't know why, but this seemed a bit odd to me. My grandmother started then, telling a story about when she was a girl. I had no idea what the story was about or why it was funny. It was not a past I knew or even cared about, but even so I wanted to hear it. I knew then, that I didn't love my grandmother. I knew because for those few moments when everything and everyone had gathered about her story, I did love her. And when her story was over, I stopped loving her again.

There was a map on the wall and I ran my eye along it. Parkgate. Joyce Bridge. Four Courts. Fishamble. There were others too and then it stopped at East Wall. I did not know where my grandmother was taking me. Or if she would stay with me when we got there. Or dump me at the door. I wasn't even sure if I trusted her at all.

I came down the steps and took a place beside her. I could smell her skin and her hair. I could smell the vanilla of the buns in her brown bag. It made me feel hungry and sick at the same time.

Welcome Home Etty

Rachael English

Etty Daly was not expected to live. Of course, no one said as much. And, even if they did, it was unlikely she would hear.

She was in a strange world, between waking and dreaming, and listening was hard. The special clothes worn by the doctors and nurses didn't help. They shuffled around the ward like blue plastic monsters. Their mouths were hidden by masks. Goggles covered their eyes. Their hats reminded her of big shower caps.

She did catch the occasional word. 'Advanced,' she heard and 'difficult'. She would try to focus on what this meant then she would fall asleep again.

Etty had never liked hospitals. Six years ago, her husband, Paddy, had nipped out to buy a newspaper. On the way home, he had a heart attack. He had been dead before the ambulance arrived. Fifty-five years of marriage, good and bad, had ended without warning. Still, if you asked her, that was the way to go. No treatments or tubes. No fuss.

When her head was clear enough to think, she wondered if she might be ready to let go. After all, who would miss her? At eighty-seven, she'd already had a longer life than many.

Her son and daughter, now middle-aged themselves, were always busy. Ivan, who liked to think he knew best, wanted her to move into a nursing home.

'We can sell the house,' he said.

And you can enjoy an early inheritance, she thought.

After the positive test, when she'd still been able to speak, Etty had called her daughter. Always kind hearted, Michelle had become tearful. Ivan had become ratty. He wanted to know where she had caught the virus. In the shop? On the bus? At Mass?

The following day, she'd taken a turn for the worse. Her temperature had soared, and she needed a machine to help her breathe. After that, the days and nights had blurred together. Despite the drugs, every part of her ached. It was hard to think of an upside, but at least she was safe from Ivan's questions.

Although she liked to think her friends would miss her, she could not be sure. She had known some of them for more than sixty years. But, after Paddy's death, the bonds between them had loosened. Their pity had been hard to disguise, and Etty didn't like pity. It was bad for the soul. She had started saying no to their invitations, and the phone calls had dried up.

She hadn't always been the quiet type. As a young woman, she had sung in a band, Etty and the Diamonds. She could see the pink contented faces. The girls with starched skirts and back-combed hair. The sweat dripping down the ballroom walls. She saw herself. Blonde hair piled high, shiny buttons on her green satin dress, white stilettos on her feet. She had never been foolish enough to believe the crowd was there for her. They had been there for a night out, a stomp and a smooch. All the same, she had relished the stage.

She had given it up when she married Paddy. That was the way, back then. Nowadays, people mocked the showbands, but they'd had their glory days. The images were still there, like a slideshow in her head.

Michelle's daughter, Clara, liked listening to Etty's stories about her singing career. Clara was a star. She ran her own hair salon in the middle of the town and often gave Etty a free wash and blow dry. Despite her hard work, she could not afford a home of her own. Along with her four-year-old son, Jack, she lived in a small flat over the salon.

Gradually, Etty realised she was getting better. She grew more aware of what was happening around her. Some of the machines were taken away, and she moved to another ward.

She asked one of the doctors how long she had spent in intensive care.

'Four weeks,' he said. 'I don't like to use the word "miracle". But, in your case, Mrs Daly, I think it's allowed.'

Not only did Etty feel stronger, her mind began to move more quickly. There was one thing she knew for sure: she was not ready for the big wooden box. Not yet. Neither did she want to be shunted off to a home. Already, Ivan was making noises about her not being well enough to live on her own.

None of the family could visit, but she talked to some of them, including Clara, every day. That was when the idea came to her.

Everyone was there as she left the hospital. The doctors and nurses, porters and cleaners. They all clapped as if she had secured a great victory, which, in a way, she had. She thought of the others who had spent time on the same ward and had not been so lucky.

Clara drove her home. When the car rounded the corner, Etty couldn't believe her eyes. Everyone was out on the street. They stood two metres apart, waving and carrying balloons. Her next door neighbours had put up a huge sign. 'Welcome Home Etty' it said. That the letters looked to have been painted by their children made it all the lovelier.

Stepping inside was wonderful. For a long time, she had feared she would never see home again. The house was like an old friend.

Etty was relaxing in her favourite chair when Ivan arrived. He was carrying a bunch of lilies, which she always thought were better suited to funerals.

She didn't have to wait long for his announcement.

'I've been looking at some homes, Mam,' he said. 'Good places. You won't need to be on your own.'

Etty and Clara swapped a look.

'She won't be on her own,' said Clara. 'Jack and I are coming to live here. We will be moving in tomorrow.'

'That's right,' said Etty, with what she hoped was her sweetest smile. 'It's all arranged. Now, make yourself useful, Ivan pet, and put on the kettle. I'm parched.'

The Other City

Patrick Freyne

The Other City is just across the bay from this one and the people come over here often enough. They are taller and paler than us and they dress in black. They smile all the time and they do not say much. They just stare at us.

We tend to act as if they are not there. Just today I was sitting with Joe discussing a better supply chain for paper cups – our company makes paper cups – when I noticed a group of visitors from the Other City in the corner. I stopped talking about flow charts for a moment.

'Why do they stare?' I whispered. Joe, who clearly had not been listening to my presentation, looked up from his notes drowsily.

'Oh, just ignore them,' he said. And I did. That is what we generally do with the people from the Other City.

Every day we pass them by on the street or in the office without comment. We try not to notice them as we brush our teeth and go to bed. They never get in the way, to be fair. Even in my small one-bedroom flat, I can move around them just fine.

I'm not incurious. Sometimes as I lie in bed I can feel their eyes on me in the darkness and I feel like asking them a question. The question sits on the tip of my tongue but I never ask it. There is a reason we don't ask them questions but I cannot remember what it is.

Here is what I know.

The Other City has always been there. It is a bit brighter, a bit taller, and a bit cleaner than our city. I seem to remember the Other City being there when I was a child. And I remember the people from the Other City quietly watching at all the key points of my life. At my childhood dinner table, at birthday parties. At school fun days. When I clumsily lost my virginity. When I started my first job. When I designed my first paper cup. When I devised a supply chain for paper cups with Joe.

At each instance, the Other City shone from across the water and its people, with their long, white, smiling faces, looked on. I suppose I like them being there. I suppose I would miss them if they were gone.

I'm really not incurious. I'm not. I do wonder why anyone would build two cities so close together. I wonder why the people from the Other City come here but we never go there. I wonder why, when I see old maps at the subway station, my city is not on a bay at all but looks straight out on open water. In those maps there is no Other City.

I sometimes wonder about other cities that are not the Other City. There are names in my head 'Paris', 'London', 'New York', 'Dublin'. I've never heard those names. And yet I know them in my head.

Life is just so busy. When I think about learning more about the Other City, I feel overwhelmed by the details of the day. And the hustle and bustle of the street. I suppose I need some 'work-life-balance'. I feel tired all the time, to tell you the truth. When I am not working, all I want to do is sleep.

'All I want to do is sleep,' I say to Joe, as we work on improving the supply chain for paper cups. 'Were we always this tired?'

Joe looks up from his notebook. He looks sleepy too. Sometimes he says: 'We were always this tired.' And sometimes he says: 'We are more tired than we were before.'

The gist of it is that Joe is not particularly interested in this line of conversation. But whatever he says, the people from the Other City lean in to listen. They listen eagerly with their long faces and their long teeth. And their eyes get rounder and I feel wearier still.

Here is something I do not remember, something I *strongly* do not remember. I do not remember a day when I and everyone else were shocked into stillness by a shining city looming up from nothing and nowhere across the sea. I do not remember dropping my coffee and bun on the ground and screaming. I do not remember Joe's jaw opening and closing and opening and closing again. I do not remember him calling for his mother. I do not remember a young woman gripping onto my arm with fear. I do not remember a baby crying and then everyone crying. I do not remember my legs getting weak as we all stared at the Other City. And the smiling white-faced strangers walked slowly into the crowd. I do not remember that at all, thank God.

The Writer who Lives in a Suitcase

Yan Ge

Years ago, when I was writing in Chinese, I was invited by the University of Leeds to be a speaker at their writing workshop. My translator picked me up from Heathrow. We took the tube to King's Cross and then the train to Yorkshire. It was almost winter. When we stepped out of Leeds train station, my translator suggested we get a taxi.

The driver was a red-cheeked man with a heavy accent. 'You ladies any plan for the visit?' he asked.

'We are going to the university, for a literature event,' my translator said.

'Oh! A literature event?' he said and looked at us from the rear-view mirror.

'Yes, and we have a very important writer here in this taxi,' my translator announced.

'Oh really?' he looked at us again.

Later we arrived at the hotel and the driver came to help us with our luggage. My translator's suitcase was a small one because she was only staying for two nights. Mine was big and heavy because I had come from China and would stay for a week. The driver lifted my translator's suitcase and then mine. 'Oh!' he exclaimed. 'This is heavy! What's in there?' he asked.

'That very important writer,' I said.

I told this story the next day at the workshop to show the students the beauty of a plot twist. It was a very successful event. We laughed a lot, then went to a local Chinese restaurant and drank lots of wine.

Ironically, only a few months later, I became a writer who lives in a suitcase, for real.

To be honest, it wasn't too bad living in a suitcase. It was basically a studio. One whole space well designed and neat. At the beginning, it felt a bit cramped but once I got used to it, it was in fact, pretty spacious. It was not a bad place to sleep and certainly a fine spot to have dinner without being interrupted. When the weather was good, the sunshine came in through a crack (bless the crack). I could even boil up the kettle to make myself a nice cup of tea. And, did I mention the solitude? Ah the solitude one can enjoy being inside of a suitcase. The best thing that could ever happen to a writer.

When I was a child, my favourite thing to do was to hide in the narrow gap between the closet and the sofa in my parents' bedroom. One day, when I was sitting in the gap enjoying my solitude, my mother came back. She looked very upset so she didn't notice I was there, between the closet and the sofa. She was accompanied by a strange man. I could not recall the man's face but I remembered he had a red nose. They went to the living room and started to talk. After a while, my mother began to cry. I remembered I was very concerned. I tried to decide if I should go out to comfort her or not. I did not go. The red-nosed man said something. Then he left. My mother was in the living room by herself. At this point, I started to feel scared. I decided to stay in the gap.

I could not tell how long my mother sat there and cried. It probably felt much longer to me than it really was. Eventually she finished. She stood up. I could hear her open a drawer and take something out.

And then she left.

She took off on that day and never came back. When I realised she was gone for good I tried to tell my father about the red-nosed man. About their conversation in the living room. But he said: 'What are you talking about? Your mother died.' I could not believe what he said. However, everybody else seemed to agree with him.

'Poor little girl, you must be so confused. Your Mama passed away. It was such a tragedy,' they said.

'But no,' I tried to argue, 'I saw her there, quarrelling with a red-nosed man …'

'Oh,' my relative reached out her hand and stroked my hair. 'You poor thing. She just died.'

That was what they said. They said my mother passed away when I was little. They said the story I tried to tell them was just my imagination. They said I read too much fiction so I could not tell reality from fantasy. They said: '… but it is great that it worked out for you and now you are a writer! It is a blessing from your Mama!'

That was what they said anyway.

Maybe I should talk about how I ended up in the suitcase. It was not long after I returned home from

74

THE WRITER WHO LIVES IN A SUITCASE

England when the real winter came. It was the most difficult winter I could remember. My grandmother said that was how I always felt in the middle of any winter. 'Do you remember the winter when you were just eleven?' she asked. I could not remember. But I did know this particular one was nasty. It was cold, humid, dark. And it was, for the first time, heavily polluted.

When the smog came we thought it was just fog. But soon we realised it was far more ferocious than fog. It darkened the cold, made the air dense and made the sun disappear. My father commented when he was drinking, 'Look at how dusty this table gets! I just cleaned it this morning!' His friend, who was drinking with him, said: 'A real man is not built for table-cleaning. Old Xu, you need to get yourself a woman.'

My father frowned and said: 'What do I need a woman for?'

The friend said, 'Old Xu, you are kidding! A woman can do a million kinds of things. She cleans and cooks. She could take care of you and your child. And she could certainly do a lot more in the bedroom! You see, nowadays it is dark all day, you could both go to bed early and …' My father slapped his friend and the friend laughed.

There were other jokes about the smog. Some were hilarious, some not so funny. But people laughed over them regardless since the jokes were free. They also laughed at the young hipsters who made a fuss out of the smog. People who checked the Air Quality Index every day and wore face masks.

My grandmother, who was eighty-five, went to the market one day and saw a group of kids wearing what looked like white gas masks. She was scared. She asked me, 'What is happening these days with you kids? Is there a war coming?' I explained to her they were probably students from a nearby college. They wore masks because of the air pollution.

My grandmother was confused. She checked outside of the window and said: 'Air pollution? What are you talking about? It is just cloudy. It is always cloudy here. You kids of this generation are so spoiled, coming up with all this nonsense! You know what? Back in my day, everybody was starving. I had no meat for six years. Those were the real tough days ...'

She was right. None of these young students had ever been starved, beaten or persecuted. Unlike their parents and grandparents, they had never seen the war, the famine or the revolution. We considered them privileged, therefore arrogant and ungrateful.

I had a bad cold around the New Year's holiday when my father came home. He asked me about the protest.

'What protest?' I asked.

'Those college students!' he scowled. 'They are protesting on the street and blocked all the traffic! My tour bus couldn't get through. I had to detour around the second ring road. Such chaos!'

'What are they protesting about?' I asked.

'The air pollution! They want the government to shut down the new factory up in the mountain. Like that will ever happen! Those trouble makers! Now we are all ordered to not go outside! Do they have any idea how much money my agency is going to lose from this?' He was upset and called his friends to come over and have a drink.

They came and sat around the table drinking and joking, eating roasted pig ears.

No matter how loud their laughter, the tragic reality would not transform itself into a comedy. A few days later my father and I went to visit grandmother but only found her empty apartment.

'Ma!' my father shouted, 'Ma! Where are you?'

'She is not here.' I checked the bedroom, kitchen and bathroom.

'Where could she go? She cannot go outside these days!' my father said, concerned. 'I'm going to call the police! Something is wrong!' He took out his phone.

'Don't call the police!' Suddenly, we heard grandmother's voice. 'Come here,' the voice said. It came from grandfather's old bedroom. We dashed into the bedroom, which had been turned into a storage room after grandfather died.

'Nainai!' I called out, 'Nainai!'

'I'm here!' I heard her voice, coming from this big wooden chest by the nightstand.

'Why are you in the chest?' My father stepped forward. 'I'll open this for you now!'

'Don't! Don't!' she shouted, 'I'm fine here. I'm living here now.'

Later, we learned my grandmother was not the first and certainly not the last to retreat into an enclosed compartment. The government declared them weak-minded traitors of our beliefs. But we all knew, the truth was, these people had to find a place to hide from the smog. This time my father could not laugh. He frowned and sighed and smoked quite a few cigarettes.

'Are you OK, Dad?' I asked him.

'Don't go out these days. I'll order an air purifier,' he said.

One sunny morning before the air purifier arrived my father cooked poached eggs and came to my room to tell me the breakfast was ready. He found that I was not in my bed, that my bedroom was empty.

I could never know how he felt when he heard my voice rising from the red suitcase. I was not able to see his face, but he walked away in silence.

Cell 13

Carlo Gébler

'My sleep's banjaxed,' said Ricky from the doorway of cell 13.

'Why is that?' I asked. I was in the corridor outside, buffing the linoleum with the polisher. One of my orderly duties. 'Guilty conscience?'

He had knocked a bloke unconscious in a club. Thrown him off the fire escape to the car park forty feet below, and killed him. He'd copped twenty.

'No Chalky,' he said, 'because this cell's haunted.'

'What?'

'There is a presence at night.' He gestured at the cell behind. 'TB hanged himself in here, didn't he?'

I nodded. I was on the wing when it happened. 'But none of the guys who had your cell since then, or before you,' I said, 'ever spoke of "a presence".'

'Whatever,' said Ricky. 'But there is, and it's doing my head in.'

'What does it look like, this presence?'

'Are you mad?' he said. 'You think I look? I hide under my covers until morning unlock.'

I saw an opportunity. Why not take it? I thought. I could make something here. 'Four pouches of Golden Virginia and five phone cards and I'll swap cells,' I said. I was in cell 1, further along. 'Just square it with the screws.'

Ricky went down to the officers' pod to ask. Five minutes later I was summoned there. Inside I found Ricky with Hayes, a day screw.

'Chalky, you are an agnostic, right?' said Hayes. 'So you don't do ghosts?'

Whatever I thought about ghosts it had nothing to do with being agnostic, which I had always thought was not being sure about God and if He existed. I did not correct him though. I had too much riding on this.

'Ricky here,' said Hayes, 'is not happy with his accommodation. Normally we don't move inmates at their request. But if the orderly asks, that's different. I take it you are requesting a cell swap?'

'Yes.'

'Lovely. Let's do the paperwork, make it official.'

Every cell has a television and when you move into a cell you sign a contract for that TV. You agree to pay fifty pence a week. If you smash it, you agree to continue paying but with no replacement set until you've paid ten quid. This stops prisoners smashing their sets if they riot.

Hayes tore up our old contracts and wrote new ones. We signed. Then we swapped our clobber. I was now the official occupant of cell 13.

* * *

I turned in at eleven and fell asleep. I awoke a few hours later. There was a sound, watery and scratchy.

I raised my head. The cell light was off but the security lights outside shone through the bars. I saw the outlines of my table, television, cell door, hand basin, and the partition that screens the toilet. I needed light but the switch at the door was too far away.

Then I had a brainwave. I slipped the remote from its place under my pillow, pressed 'On' and jumped up. The set came on and by the light from the screen I saw, slithering over the toilet rim, having swum up the U-bend, a rat.

'Christ!' The rat sprang to the floor and ran under the table on which the TV sat. Jesus. From the

82

bed – I wasn't getting down – I leaned across to the control panel by the cell door, and hit the light and the alarm. I heard the bell ringing faintly in the officers' pod. I banged on the cell door.

'There's a rat in my cell,' I shouted.

I retreated to the middle of my bed. The rat scurried to the wardrobe. There was food on the top shelf. Ah.

I reached over, found a tin of sweet corn and hurled it. Missed. I found another tin and flung it. He got himself into the corner by the door. As far as he could get from me in an eight-by-five-foot cell. There were footfalls outside. My bell stopped. It had been turned off using the switch outside. The flap over the Judas slit lifted.

'What?' the night screw shouted in.

'There's a rat in here.'

'What do you expect me to do about it?'

'Unlock the door.'

'And let it onto the wing?'

'You have to do something.'

Philly in the cell opposite was now awake, woken by the commotion.

'Get a dog, then unlock the cell,' he shouted. 'The dog will get it.'

'Good plan,' said the night screw.

'No,' I said, 'unlock the cell now.'

'Can't,' said the night screw. 'The keys are in the control room.'

I remembered. They did not keep keys on the landings at night. The night screw went off.

'Hey, Chalky,' shouted Philly, 'got any chocolate?'

'What?'

'Rats love chocolate. Throw a square onto the floor, wait till he comes. When he does, drop your telly on him.'

Nothing else for it, I thought.

I leaned over, unplugged the set and lifted it onto my bed. The rat watched. I pulled a bar of Cadbury's Fruit and Nut from the wardrobe shelf. I broke out four squares and dropped them on the floor below my bed. Then I picked up the set.

After a pause the rat moved to the chocolate and began to scrape it with his large white teeth. I dropped the set. There was a sound of splintering plastic and breaking glass.

'Victory?' Philly shouted.

'I think so.'

Philly pushed his bell and the night screw returned.

'No need for the dog,' shouted Philly.

'Success?' the night screw shouted in.

'Just get the key.'

Time passed. The night screw returned and unlocked the door. He had a broom. He used this to ease the TV back. There was my chocolate, and there was the rat. Its eyes had popped out.

'You know I'll have to report you for smashing your TV,' he said.

'Obviously.'

* * *

Hayes called me down to the pod the following morning. A dusty TV sat on his desk.

'You smashed your in-cell TV,' he said. 'Model inmate like you, I'm shocked.'

He blew dust off the set on his desk.

'Incidentally,' Hayes continued, 'I do know what an agnostic is. It means … well, being flexible … like me.'

He blew more dust off.

'I think this was an extra set that never went back to stores,' he said. 'It was in the cupboard. Anyhow, I have amended your contract. That is now officially cell 13's set. Pop it down please.'

Careful Lady Driver
Ciara Geraghty

She paid for me in cash. I was her first. I sensed her pride, despite her initial reservations about my colour. Some might call it garish and I concede that there are many colours duller than I. Ronald, the salesman, wore a shiny suit. Pastry-white pouches of skin oozed between the buttons of his loud shirt. No, he told her. I was not mustard. I was gold.

I was only six back then. A six-year-old golden Nissan Micra. One previous owner, Ronald said. Which was not the case. I don't like to speak out of turn but used-car salesmen can be deserving of their reputation, in my experience.

She stuck an L-plate on my rear window, even though she had passed her test back in Dublin, first time round. London was not an easy city to navigate. That was what she told people when they wondered about the learner sticker.

She was a hesitant driver. The cautious press of her feet on my pedals. The grip of her hands on my steering wheel.

She met him on her second weekend in London. He was older. Her first grown-up lover. He liked to show her off. He brought her to the vintage car shows he often attended. He took her for lunch in traditional English pubs. He would sit her by the window, like an ornament on display. He rarely agreed to travel in my modest interior. When he did, he insisted on driving. He complained about the shrill rasp of my engine, no matter how much oil he administered. And it is true that the engine of his company car purred like a stroked cat.

When she got her promotion, he said she should buy a new car. She did not dismiss his suggestion. Nor did she pursue it wholeheartedly.

She moved from her basement studio flat in Camden into his two-bed ground floor apartment in Battersea. She wondered where the coin-operated electricity meter was. He performed an indulgent smile and called her adorable.

'You make me feel safe,' she whispered to him across my faux-leather seats as he drove her few possessions to his place.

He liked things to be pristine and ordered. I daresay this was connected to his brief and, I imagine, earnest stint in the army. Take the deliberation with which he took to my bonnet and hood at dawn every Saturday morning. He used a soft shammy. I can still see the expression on his face, reflected in my windows. Alert and dogged, the corner of his fleshy tongue trapped between his furiously scrubbed teeth. She teased his exacting care but there was a wistfulness in her voice.

She called me Mo. Short for Motor perhaps. I did not mind the name. It had an affectionate tone. It was in keeping with the essence of her – an enduring innocence, despite everything.

He could not believe she did not know how to iron. He was appalled at her untidiness. He did not like when she ribbed him gently about the row of his spotlessly clean shirts in the wardrobe – lined up like soldiers on parade.

Monday was laundry day, he had declared early on. Sometimes she went out instead. This caused arguments. He did not like her drinking on a Monday night. He did not like her going out without him. She told him he did not own her. He told her he was protecting her.

One Monday night, she parked me outside a pizzeria. Later, I spotted him, across the road. The shadows gave him cover. He stood there for over an hour. His eyes were trained on the window of the restaurant. Through the glass, he could see her with her work mates. Her fork trailed spaghetti as she moved it towards her mouth. When she laughed, she threw her head back. Her hair, loose and tumbling down her back, attracted admiring glances. She looked younger that night. I was the nervous one, truth be told. Perhaps because of how still he stood. Or how long he stood, watching. The darkness covered him like a shroud. And something about the might and power of his body unnerved me. There was a thrum to it, like an electric fence.

He wanted her every night. She asked him why he never looked at her face when they had sex. He sometimes left presents for her to find on the passenger seat: teddy suits, peep-hole bras, suspender belts. They were wrapped in delicate tissue paper, inside discreet brown paper bags. He was strict about their diet and exercise plans. When he found the chocolate bar and crisp wrappers in my glove compartment, he stiffened. He released his hot breath slowly. Like a parent discovering trails of jam from sticky fingers along newly painted walls. He arranged the wrappers on the dashboard in a tidy line.

He did not like her smoking. He said it looked vulgar. He hung a 'Thank You For Not Smoking' sign on my rear-view mirror. And he reminded her with his tone of strained patience, his mother had died of lung cancer. She left the sign there.

Once, when he was away on business, she leaned out the sash window of their apartment and chain-smoked. She smoked until the packet was empty.

Sometimes, on the way home from work, she would park at the end of a narrow cul-de-sac. It was near their apartment but could not be seen. She did not have to worry there about him passing by.

She would get out and sit on the kerb, exhaling in long, shaky breaths. I worried about her on those nights. Alone and exposed in a darkening city. It is true that she was a tall girl. A woman I should say. In her mid-twenties perhaps. A mane of long, coppery red hair that she often fought with. She had no idea how random drivers stared at her when she stopped at the lights. I imagined they marvelled at the way her hair glinted gold where the sun touched it. How it framed her small, pale face with the freckles she hated. When she looked up, the colour of her eyes could appear bright blue or gunmetal grey, depending on the day.

That last morning, the colour was difficult to make out. Her eyelids were puffy and the skin beneath her eyes was dark – like inky finger prints.

She flinched at her reflection in the rear-view mirror. She spread her cold fingers on my dashboard, the surface warming as the sun picked itself out of the horizon. It was a small offering on my part but one I was glad to provide.

He made a performance of manhandling the largest box out of the apartment. I could not help overhearing their argument last night. The window was open. He told her she did not have the guts to leave. It is true that the manner of her packing was sluggish and unconvincing. He threw a glance at her. She stayed where she was, not looking at him. He shoved the box into the back seat, balancing it on the suitcase she arrived in London with, five years earlier. There was a seat belt secured about its middle now. The alloy clasps not as dependable as they once were.

'I managed to fit everything in,' he said.

She wound down the window. He dipped his head through the frame and cupped her face with his hands. For a moment, I worried that she might stay. A harbour, no matter how exposed, can seem safer than the open sea.

She turned the key.

The laminated A4 sheet with directions to Holyhead lay on the passenger seat. She drove in silence. Her familiar feet pressed against my pedals as we made our way out of London. The glass and brick of the high rises receded in my rear-view mirror. When they disappeared, she cried.

Up ahead, a lay-by. She pulled in and got out. She paced up and down, breathing hard. After a while, she stopped. She stared through my windows, perhaps dwelling on the boxes, perhaps thinking about their contents. A hairdryer. A collection of poetry she bought in a second-hand bookshop – never read. The spoils of their DVD tug-of-war. The first work suit she had purchased with her first overdraft. The trappings of her twenties.

But it was the L-plate that had caught her attention. She had to open the boot to get at it. A box, crippled with shoes, fell onto the ground.

She picked at the edge of the sticker with her nails. It was stuck fast. Eventually, one of the corners relented. She tightened her fingers around the tiny curl and pulled. It made a ripping sound. She balled it between her palms, took out her lighter. The plastic melted and curdled, emitting a toxic smell. She doused it with water before dropping it into a bin. When she got back into the car, she wound down all the windows. She lit a cigarette and turned on the radio. Turned it all the way up.

* * *

I have changed hands a few times since then. Always advertised as the car of a careful lady driver. But that was true only once, a long time ago now.

I have now been sold to a scrapyard by a wafer-thin, freshly divorced plumber who was finally relieved of his driver's licence.

He told the judge the licence was all he had left. She said he should have taken better care of it then.

It is only a matter of time now. I suppose we all have this coming to us, sooner or later. My golden hue has dulled over the years. Rust has taken the upper hand for the most part – mainly around my undercarriage area.

But there was a moment, back then, when I flashed down a motorway. My windows wound all the way down. The radio turned all the way up.

Carrying a young woman away from something.
Except it did not feel like we were leaving.

It felt like we were going someplace, she and I.

We were on our way.

The Tatty Hoker

Ruth Gilligan

He drove the rental car out of the airport and over the old roads. At first they had planned to take the ferry, but he worried that it would be too hard on her delicate stomach. Inside his head, the noise of the propellers was still very loud. At least it meant the ghosts were quiet for a while.

The B&B had orange curtains and purple heather in a pot. She said she thought that it looked charming. He carried their bags in from the boot. The woman at Reception had hazel eyes. She found their reservation in a giant book. He wanted to tell her that it was the first time a stranger had written their names down like that.

Mr & Mrs.

She showed them to the living room. She had prepared a tray of tea. 'You must be very thirsty after your journey?'

He stared at the pictures on the walls. They were mostly black and white photographs. Inside his head, the ghosts were back again.

'Is it your first time in Scotland?' She held out a plate of biscuits.

His wife took one. 'Martin came when he was a boy. Potato picking,' she said.

'Oh really?'

He cracked his knuckle. 'We are on our honeymoon.'

'How exciting!' She put the plate down.

The women discussed finger food and lace. Outside the window, it began to rain.

All the Galway lads used to take the boat to Scotland for the summer. They spent their days sweating in the fields. They spent their nights sleeping in the sheds. For him it was all worth it because he got to be with his father again. His father who lived over here for eleven months of the year. Apparently there just was not enough work back home. Apparently there were just too many men and too few crops.

After they unpacked, it was still raining. The view from the bedroom was pretty grey. He worried that she would suspect he had only chosen this place because of his own agenda.

'Shall we take a nap?' She turned her back to him while she undressed. They were still shy with one another. He lay there and watched her while she slept.

Those summers he had watched his father too, living his other life. Chatting with the locals in Gaelic and smiling at everyone. He seemed to be friendly with the couple who owned the biggest farm. Supposedly the wife was learning English, so his father gave her lessons.

She wore a pink dress to dinner. Downstairs, another woman showed them to their table. She said that she was the owner's sister. Her eyes were bright blue, the same as his. 'Agnes tells me that you are Irish? That you were a *tatty hoker*?'

'A what?'

'A potato picker.' She poured two glasses of water. 'Did you come over on your own?'

He explained how his father had lived here for most of the year. 'Until he died,' he said. 'In a fire in '68.'

The jug slipped from her hand and the water poured all over his wife's pink lap. He reached across with his napkin, but it was too late.

The next morning, he woke early. He got dressed very quietly. In the bathroom, he stared at their toothbrushes standing side by side. He felt guilty about sneaking off, but he told himself that it was all for her. He would be a better husband if he could make the ghosts in his head finally shut up.

Downstairs, the sister was there. He pretended to be surprised. He explained that he wanted to visit the cottage where his father used to stay. Outside, the rain had stopped, but the grass was still damp. They walked in silence. He noticed that her hair was the same colour as his too.

He saw the ruins from afar. The ground was charred in a black rectangle. There was a small pile of stones and the burnt remains of some wooden planks. After his father died, his mother didn't let him come to Scotland again. Not even to try and find some answers. There were rumours about the fire, but nobody knew for certain how it had started.

'I used to get nightmares.' He took a deep breath. The land around them smelled of mulch and rot. 'I would see him calling out and then I would see the flames.' He didn't tell her that he was glad when the nightmares stopped, but then he was sad because he missed his father's face. He didn't tell her about the ghosts.

Agnes's sister took her hands from her pockets. She stared at the horizon while she spoke. 'I once asked my mammy what happened, but she said that she didn't know. She was in hospital at the time, pregnant with me. The following week, my daddy sold the farm and ran away to England.' She sighed. In the daylight, the resemblance was uncanny.

He waited for a moment while all the pieces fell into place. 'Out of interest, how was your mammy's English?'

This time she stared at him. 'Fluent, why?'

He expected to feel angry, but instead he felt only relief. 'So your father was a jealous man?'

She also waited for a moment. 'I suppose that he was. And I suppose that yours was a very good teacher?'

When they returned, his wife was in the breakfast room eating on her own. She was cutting a bit of rasher. Maybe her stomach wasn't delicate anymore.

'I'm back.' He wanted to tell her that he had found answers. He wanted to tell her that he had found a half-sister too. Instead, he sat down and ordered himself a fry.

They spoke a little while they drank their coffee. They made plans for the day ahead. He thought how she would be pregnant soon and how he wouldn't run away. Otherwise, inside his head, everything was silent. His breakfast came with hash browns. The potatoes were fried golden and sweet.

Spirit Animals

Emily Hourican

'I had a dream about you last night.'

At the sound of Juliette's voice, Sarah's shoulders tightened with tension.

'You had a dream about me, Aunt Juliette?' Joe asked. He was eating cereal. He put down his spoon. 'What dream?'

'I dreamed of a snow wolf.' Juliette leaned closer to the little boy. Her voice dropped low. 'The snow wolf was running and leaping through deep, white snow. Glad to be alive.'

'Where was I?' Joe asked.

'You were the snow wolf. So now I know. A snow wolf is your spirit animal. And Joe, it is an incredibly powerful spirit animal. It means you have an appetite for freedom.'

Sarah wished there was a polite way to tell someone who sat in your kitchen and lived in your house to shut up. Not just someone though. Juliette. Juliette was her husband Richard's younger sister. She had dark purple hair and the word 'fearless' tattooed on the inside of her arm. Juliette had come to live with them six months ago, after yet another failed relationship.

'What is a spirit animal?' Joe asked.

Sarah closed the lunchbox with a snap. 'Joe, finish your breakfast. You need to hurry for school,' she said.

'Your spirit animal is the shape of your soul,' Juliette said. 'It is your guide and helper in this world but also in the other world.'

'Joe, come on.' Sarah felt irritated by Juliette's silly talk, so her voice was snappish. Joe looked up at her too fast and said 'What's wrong?'

'Nothing,' Sarah said. 'Nothing's wrong. But we are going to be late.'

'Ok,' Joe said. 'What is your spirit animal?' he asked Juliette.

'A black panther,' Juliette said.

'Of course it is,' muttered Sarah to herself. No way was it going to be a mouse or a sparrow.

She went upstairs. Richard was tying his tie. 'She's supposed to be looking for a job,' Sarah said. 'But all she ever does is meditate and cook horrible desserts made with coconut sugar.'

'I know,' he said. 'I buy the ingredients. They cost a fortune.'

'So stop buying them. She can buy her own. We're not making her pay rent, because she's your sister and you feel sorry for her.'

'Sarah, she can't afford to. You know she can't,' Richard said.

'But it has been months, and she doesn't show signs of ever leaving.'

'Give her time. She is so good with Joe. He loves having her here.'

'She fills his head with nonsense,' Sarah said. 'She talks to him about his aura, the healing power of the mind. How he can do anything if he visualises it.'

'But he likes it.'

'Maybe, but it's not good for him. He should be outside, playing with other children, not in with her painting pictures of his aura.'

Back downstairs Sarah picked up Joe's coat. 'We're off,' she called from the front door. She wondered would Juliette clear away the breakfast things. Or leave them there for Sarah to do when she got back from work.

In the car on the way to school, Sarah tried to prepare Joe for the day ahead. This was what his teacher, Miss Ryan, had suggested she do, at their last meeting. She said it would help Joe to 'settle.'

'You have your hurl and helmet,' Sarah said. 'It's hurling practice today.'

'Yes.'

'And you have reading in the morning, before Little Break.'

'OK.'

The way he didn't complain hurt Sarah more than if he had protested. She felt she was driving a small, scared prisoner who had learned not to thrash or fuss. Every day when she arrived at pick-up time he was waiting for her, his bag on his shoulders. Around him, other children played. Not Joe.

'Let's go,' he always said as soon as he saw her.

'Juliette says my spirit animal is a snow wolf,' Joe said now, proudly. 'And hers is a black panther. What's yours?'

'I have no idea,' Sarah said. 'I don't really believe in that stuff.'

'But if it is real?' he persisted. 'What would you be?'

'I don't know, maybe a chicken.'

'You wouldn't be a chicken,' he said, offended on her behalf. 'Maybe Juliette knows what you are.'

'It's just stories,' she said. 'Juliette doesn't know.'

At the gates, she kissed him goodbye. 'I love you, darling. See you later. Have a good day.'

'See you later.' He never said he loved her at the drop-offs.

Sarah watched him walk across the playground alone. She wanted to run after him, grab the bag from his back and say 'not today! Let's go somewhere else, just us.' She wanted to hold him tight. To be the person who protected him, not the person who dropped him every morning to a school he hated. How much longer would they give it, she wondered as she drove on to work. Another month? A year? And then what?

'He will settle,' Richard had said, after the first meeting with Joe's teacher, Miss Ryan, a few months in to Junior Infants. That was when Miss Ryan said they should have Joe 'assessed'. In case he had 'additional needs.'

'He just needs time,' Richard had said. 'He's young for his age.'

Sarah had agreed 'He is. Nearly the youngest in the class …' But she knew that it was not just his youth that set Joe apart. It was something else, something that was in him, that made the other children want to hurt him, not help him.

EMILY HOURICAN

'Let's go,' Joe said as soon as he saw Sarah that afternoon. But before they could leave, Miss Ryan came over to them.

'Can I speak to you?' she asked. She put a hand on Sarah's arm to stop her from leaving.

'Yes, of course,' Sarah said. Her heart sank. 'Joe, wait here for me.'

The classroom smelled of chalk and feet and disinfectant.

'There was an incident during hurling practice,' Miss Ryan said. 'Joe hit another boy with his hurl.'

'I see.' Sarah waited. Experience had taught her that it was better to wait.

'I did not see how it began,' Miss Ryan continued. She was speaking quickly. 'Joe said that the other boy started the fight. But I asked the other children, and they said that the other boy did not do anything physical.'

No, Sarah thought, he would not have to. Not at this stage. The groundwork had been so well laid by months of teasing.

'Joe would not hit anyone without good reason,' Sarah said. 'Even then, he would have to be provoked a lot.'

'I'm sure that is true,' Miss Ryan said, 'but at this school we have a policy of no tolerance for hitting.'

106

Of course you do, thought Sarah. You have a policy for anything easy. But where is your policy for protecting a child who finds every day in your care confusing and lonely, and now dangerous?

'I was wondering,' Miss Ryan continued, 'if you have thought any more about an assessment?' Her voice was full of concern but Sarah did not believe in her concern.

'We have not,' Sarah said.

'Perhaps you should,' Miss Ryan said. Sarah knew that Miss Ryan wanted an answer that would make her own life easier. A piece of paper with a label that would tell her what to do with Joe.

'We will consider it,' Sarah said.

And they would have to, she knew. Even though she did not believe that giving Miss Ryan the label she was looking for would make her a better teacher to Sarah's son.

Outside, Sarah took Joe's hand on the way to the car. The playground was empty so he let her. She wondered would he ask what Miss Ryan had wanted. He did not. He stared out the window and said nothing until they reached the house.

'What day is it today?' he asked then.

'Tuesday,' Sarah said. 'Why?'

He did not answer, but she knew he was calculating in his head: if today is Tuesday then tomorrow is Wednesday, then it's Thursday and then Friday, and then the weekend.

Her heart ached at how much he wished the weeks away.

They went into the kitchen where Juliette was baking. She had cleared the breakfast bowls but there was cocoa powder on the pale wooden countertop. And some of those dried red berries that she ate that stuck in her teeth.

'I am making chia seed brownies,' she said, to both of them. 'Do you want to help?' she asked Joe.

'Yes please,' he said. 'Can I stir the bowl?'

She pulled a stool out for him and lifted him onto it. 'Of course you can. It's hard work, because of the chia seeds, but they have loads of protein to make you strong.'

Sarah watched them. Joe's head was bent over the bowl and he stirred the thick mixture with a wooden spoon. The mixture looked disgusting, Sarah thought. Juliette put her hand over Joe's, to help him.

'That is very good, Joe,' Juliette said. And Sarah, just as she had known that the concern in Miss

Ryan's voice was fake, heard that the love in Juliette's voice was real.

'Juliette, tell me more about Joe's spirit animal,' Sarah said. 'A snow wolf? What does that mean?'

'It's a really powerful sign,' Juliette said. Joe stopped stirring and turned his head to look at Juliette.

'Go on,' Sarah said, pulling out a stool. 'Tell me all about it.'

Where It All Began

Úna-Minh Kavanagh

The longest journey in life starts with one step.

How on earth did a little Asian girl become a proud Kerry woman, thick accent and all? It just so happens that another Kerry woman chose Vietnam to search for a child to raise as her own in 'The Kingdom'.

This is my truth. I do not have that red-haired, freckled, pale-skinned look that tourists think of when they read about Ireland. I have black hair, dark brown eyes that curve like a cat and light brown skin. That's right, I am a brown Irish woman! And if you saw me walking down an O'Connell Street anywhere in the country, you might, at a glance, take me for a tourist. Or, better still, an immigrant who has settled in Ireland.

It's true, I was not born here. In fact, I was not born anywhere near here. My story actually begins on 4 July 1991, more than 10,000 kilometres from Ireland. I was born in the city of Hanoi, the capital of Vietnam. The first part of my first name 'Úna-Minh' (pronounced 'Oona-Ming') is the Irish version of my grandmother's name, Winifred. It is also a play on the Irish word 'uan', meaning 'lamb'. The second part of my first name celebrates my Vietnamese heritage. 'Minh' is Sino-Vietnamese and means 'bright'. I am the only person in the world with the name Úna-Minh. Let's face it, I am not your usual Irish woman.

I know very little about my Vietnamese birth family. Over the years, the information about them that has come my way has been sparse and impossible to verify. In the parts of my Vietnamese birth certificate where my birth parents' names should be, I find the words 'no father' and 'no mother'. My sense of how I came to be comes from the accounts of others: Mom and the doctors and officials in the hospital where I was born. So I treat everything I've been told as a possible truth in my story.

What my mom, Noreen, knows is that my birth mother was much too poor and too young to look after me. She came from a village outside of Hanoi. And when she was pregnant with me she was unmarried. Being single and pregnant brought great shame upon her family. There was never any question of her keeping me, her daughter. Like my birth mother, generations of Irish women and girls also suffered shame and stigma in their own families and communities.

While she was pregnant, to avoid rumours, my birth mother and her own mother moved from their small village to Hanoi. A huge city with a population of over a million people at the time. It was an enormous step for them to take. They worked together in a factory along the Red River Delta making red bricks. I often wonder what it was like for my birth mother. She had to leave everything behind and work in a city so different to her home village, just to save face. Heavily pregnant in Hanoi's stifling heat, she would have mixed the red clay into rectangular shapes. As the bricks hardened, she would have carried them from one section of the factory to the other. Automated machinery had yet to come into use there.

The humidity in Vietnam, especially in the city, would make you swim in sweat. But Vietnamese women tend to wear long sleeves everywhere, to keep their skin as pale as possible. Historically, browner skin suggested working in fields and, therefore, poverty. My birth mother would have been pulling her pregnant body from one place to the other, while her arms would have been fully covered. She would have had no relief from the sweltering sun.

My mom has told me that my birth mother really didn't want to leave me when I was born. But she lived in a society where keeping up appearances was important regardless of your status. In Vietnam, the life of a woman was set in stone. You worked hard. You found a husband and married him quickly. Then, just as quickly, had children who would grow up to take care of you when you were older. For those living in poorer communities, marriages were often used to create bonds between two families. But my mother had no man, and a fatherless child. No other man would ever want to marry her.

Two days after I was born, my birth mother returned to visit me. She wanted to keep me but couldn't. It would be the last time she saw me. It was the first difficult moment in my life and it would shape my future forever.

* * *

In 1989, Noreen Kavanagh was a schoolteacher from Tralee in her early forties working in Toronto. Even though she was not in a serious relationship, she really wanted to be a mother. She thought about her options for becoming a parent on her own. Adoption made the most sense. She firmly believed that there were already so many children in the world who needed a loving and safe home. Besides, she wanted a daughter or a son, not a replica of herself!

Jacqueline was a neighbour of my mother's, from Tralee. She had been living in Hanoi, in Vietnam. She had been working with UNICEF for two years. Jacqueline was also a single woman who had adopted two Vietnamese girls. My mom would listen, fascinated and full of admiration, to Jacqueline's stories about the adoption process and how her family came to be.

When Jacqueline and her daughters came home on visits to Ireland in the 80s, Mom loved spending time with them. So, it was from Jacqueline that my mother found the courage and inspiration to adopt a child from Vietnam.

On only her second day in Vietnam, Mom was taken to one of the local hospitals, Bach Mai. The director told her a baby born three days ago was available for adoption. The baby would soon be moved to an orphanage if no adopter was found.

That baby was me.

Victoria

Louise Kennedy

I know him before he speaks. I know him by the hunch of his shoulders, by the way he tilts his glass and lowers his black and tan. He ordered it because he cannot bear to taste what they do to the Guinness here. I know before he pats his breast pocket that he will take out a packet of No. 6. They are the nearest you can get in this place to Carroll's No.1. I know he will light the cigarette with a Swan Vesta. A box of safety matches lasts no time in a damp bedsit.

Beside me, the man sits up straight. I hope he does not want to talk to me. I turn and look through the window. It is cloudy from fumes and fly spray. There are National Express coaches pulling in and out of the station, slowly. My coach is at the front with HOLYHEAD written in big letters. Around the pub there are people waiting with bags. A couple in the corner, kissing. An old woman alone at a table, frowning at the paper tag of a Lipton's teabag. Four boys with long hair and guitar cases and pints of lager.

The man orders another drink. He points at my glass. 'Will you have one yourself?' he says.

'Jesus, no. I'd never make it to motorway services in Birmingham without a toilet,' I say. 'Thanks, though.' His face goes red. I feel bad for him. I say the thing all us Irish in London say when we meet. 'Are you long over?'

'1954.'

'Wow. That is a long time.' As soon as it is out I regret saying *wow*.

'Thirty-four years. It went quick at the start. Slower now though,' he says. He takes a drink.

I know him because I have seen him in a pub in Kilburn. I went there with my friends for a laugh, to see the real bog Irish in action. Not like us, with our degrees and bottles of Mexican beer. I have seen him in the dole office in Archway. He was sitting on an orange plastic seat because the room was warm and dry. The only person in the room who did not pull a number tag out of the machine. I know him from Kentish Town tube station where he asked me for a smoke one night. There were tears streaming down his face. I know him because there are thousands of Irish men like him in London.

'Yourself?' he says.

'I am here a year,' I say.

'What line of work are you in?' he says.

'I work in an office in the City.'

'Good girl yourself. You did well.'

I want to tell him I have the most boring job in the world. That my parents are annoyed I am not using my education. That I am finding it hard to settle in London. That I want to go home for good. 'It is not too bad,' I say.

'I worked on the roads,' he says.

'Do you get home often?' I say.

'1978 was the last time. For the mother's funeral. The brother's funeral this time.'

'Sorry.'

'I am the last. There is a small farm.'

'Are you going home for good?' I say.

He does not answer. I open my handbag and find my ticket. I finish my drink and stand to go. I am worried he will come with me. His jacket smells of rasher grease and mould. I don't want to sit beside him all the way to Holyhead. The last time I went home a middle-aged man from Cork pressed me against the window of the coach. He was sweating and trembling and talking to himself.

'I am heading over,' I say.

The man takes a slow sup of his pint. 'I will follow you shortly,' he says. It comes out like 'folly'.

I cross the road and stand in the queue for the coach. There are Irish people of all ages. Students, women with small children. Men like the man in the pub, in hats and old suits, too warm for a summer day. Everyone is carrying a canvas sausage bag. I find a seat beside a girl my own age. I squash my bag into the overhead rack. The driver walks the length of the aisle, counting passengers.

'There is a man coming shortly,' I say. I look out the window and wait for him to come onto the street. After a couple of minutes, the driver holds out his hands at me.

'He said he was coming,' I say.

'Sorry, love. I cannot wait for him,' he says.

The door gasps closed. I know the set of his shoulders when he comes out of the pub. Inside, he seemed taller. From up here I can see how sparse his hair is. The mottling on his scalp from working outside. He must know this is the coach he was meant to take but he does not look up. He lifts his canvas bag over his shoulder. There is a piece of paper in his hand. He looks at it for a moment and begins to tear it up. The coach swings onto the street. I watch him sprinkle the confetti he has made of his ticket home into the bin.

To Russia with Love

Sinéad Moriarty

I rinsed out my cup. My hands were shaking. I tried to control my breathing. In and out, in and out. It was not working. I did not feel calmer. John came in and put his arms around me.

'Nervous?'

I nodded, afraid to look at him in case I might begin to cry.

John carried our suitcases into the hall. I could hear him muttering a check list. 'Passports, tickets, money ...'

As I was putting the coffee jar away, I heard loud beeping from outside. Then someone banged on our front door.

'Come on you lot, hurry up!' my father shouted.

I rushed to open the door. Three cars were parked outside our house. We had been expecting just my dad to drive us to the airport. But there were three cars. Mum and my sister in one, wearing furry Russian hats. Our best friends Kate and Frank in another car, waving a 'Good Luck' banner. In the third car were John's brother and his three young sons, all whooping.

They were all beeping their car horns, shouting and cheering.

I was so moved that I could not speak. I hugged Dad and cried into the side of his hat. Thankfully the fur mopped up most of my tears.

'Thanks,' I murmured.

Dad squeezed me tight. 'We couldn't let you go to Russia to meet your baby boy without a proper send off. Everyone wanted to join in. We are all behind you, sweetheart.'

We climbed into the back of the car. My sister handed us two Russian hats. Dad drove us to the airport, followed by our friends and family. Our very own support group.

Hours later John and I landed in Moscow airport. We were immediately surrounded by porters fighting to carry our bags. It was a bit frightening.

Eventually I handed over a bunch of dollars to a man with muscles that would have made Popeye look like a stick insect. He picked up our suitcases as if they were two Tesco shopping bags. We followed him as he stomped through customs where we had our declaration form stamped. When we walked out to the arrivals area a driver was waiting for us. He drove us to a local airport. It took nearly an hour.

We boarded a very old and battered looking plane. I clung to the side of my seat as it rattled and rocked along the runway. Finally it lifted into the sky making the most god-awful racket. John, who was not a good flyer, sat pale and jittery beside me.

We spent the next two and a half hours flying to the south of Russia. When we landed, our translator, Olga, was waiting for us. She was a very serious young woman. She shook our hands. We smiled but she did not smile back. Olga drove us to Anapa, on the Black Sea, where the orphanage was.

We had decided to adopt from Russia during our adoption course. I had romantic ideas about Russia that were based on the film *Dr Zhivago*. The real Russia was very different to my fantasy. Anapa was cold and grey.

We spent the night tossing and turning in a cold, damp hotel room. Eventually I gave up on sleep and sat up in bed to read my Kindle, but I couldn't concentrate. Finally dawn broke. D-Day had arrived.

We packed our backpack with all the gifts for Viktor, our little boy. And our gifts for the staff of the children's home. We had our camera and video recorder with us as well. Olga arrived at nine sharp to collect us. I was a nervous wreck. I tried to eat breakfast, but I just felt too sick. John looked a bit green himself. This was it. We were finally going to meet our baby son.

As Olga explained what we should expect from the day, John and I sat in the back of the car holding hands. We stared down at the only photo we had of our little boy.

The children's home was a two-storey building that looked a bit run-down. Inside, the paint was peeling off the walls and it was cold and dark. We were told to wait in a big room that was filled with toys and playpens. It wasn't as bad as I had expected. Behind this room was the dormitory where all the children slept. It was a large room stuffed full of little beds and cots. Although it was old-fashioned, it was clean.

The director of the children's home showed us around. He spoke in Russian and Olga translated for us. He told us how delighted he was that we were going to meet Viktor. He promised us that Viktor was a very healthy little boy and as bright as a button. John and I sat nervously on the couch as we waited for the children to come in from breakfast.

The door burst open. About twenty children rushed in. They ranged in age from six to six months. I looked around desperately to see Viktor. Where was he? My heart was pounding in my chest. I thought I was going to faint and then I saw him. He looked just like his photo. He was crawling along the floor in the middle of the bunch. Concentrating on getting to the other side without being trampled on. I grabbed John's arm.

'There.' I pointed to the tiny little boy in the blue babygrow. John froze.

The director picked Viktor up. He spoke gently to him in Russian. Then he handed him to me. I held the little boy in my arms. He stared up at me with his huge brown eyes.

'Hello, Viktor, I'm your mummy.' I smiled and then he won my heart by smiling back. As I stood there crying and smiling, John came over. I gently handed Viktor to him.

'Hey there little fellow,' he said, as he smiled down at his son. 'Welcome to our family.'

Viktor looked up at John and then reached up and touched his face. His little hand rested on

John's cheek, and I saw my husband cry for the first time. I turned away. It was their private moment. I moved across the room and took deep breaths. I wanted to lie down and sob. We had come so far. It had been such a long, hard road that sometimes I had wondered if it was worth it. But now, seeing John holding our beautiful son, I knew it was worth every minute.

The Party
Graham Norton

'What will we do?' Max asked.

'Play games,' his mother said brightly.

Max thought about this.

'Kevin had a man to make balloon animals.'

'Did he?' Fiona did not want to hear about other parties.

'And Kate had Elsa from *Frozen*.'

'Oh.'

'Not the real Elsa,' Max explained. 'It looked like her, but she smelled.'

He pulled a face remembering how the blue shiny dress had the smell of his daddy's work shirts. It had made him sad.

'Well, we are going to make our own fun!' Fiona said giving her son a tickle under the arms. Max wriggled away. He looked uncertain.

Max was going to be seven and had never had a party before. When they had lived in the flat, there had not been space to have kids running around. Then they moved to the council house just outside the village. Fiona had looked at her new little patch of garden and thought about Max and his friends running around. Fiona, with her husband Dave and little Max. It would be perfect. But that isn't how life works.

Dave had come home from work early. He had a pain in his head. He went to bed without dinner. The next morning Fiona knew it was bad when Dave did not go to work. The doctor saw him and then there was an ambulance to the hospital up in Cork. By eleven o'clock that night he was dead.

People had been wonderful. Fiona and Max were new to the village, but they got every bit of help you might want. Food was brought. The cleaning was done. The grass got cut. All while Fiona sat holding Max as if he was a life belt and she had fallen into a deep, dark sea.

That was over a year ago. Now they were having a party. Fiona hoped it was a good idea. It was to start at three o'clock and end at six. She had sent invites to every child in Max's class. Fourteen children.

Why was she so nervous? They were children. Perhaps it was because of Max. He stared at her as if she had forgotten something. She wished that she had time to wash her hair. It was tied back in a loose pony-tail. She hoped her jeans and bright sweatshirt said 'fun mum'. Now she was unsure.

She knew that Max was worried about the house. Often, he told her about the homes he visited after school. One family had a pizza oven in the garden! She tried to explain that people lived in different houses and that was OK. Bigger was not always better.

Fiona looked around the room. Balloons on strings were tied to the back of the kitchen chairs. On the table were plates of sandwiches and sweet treats she had made herself. Paper cups sat beside two big jugs of orange squash.

'We need fizzy!' Max had protested at the supermarket. 'It has to be Coke.'

Fiona hated to say no, but so many children would drink gallons. It had to be squash. Max's face had grown red and Fiona thought he was going to cry. He did not. He just sulked until they got to the freezer section and Fiona agreed to buy an ice cream cake. It was cheaper than she had expected.

The cake was too big for her little freezer on top of the fridge. Old Mrs Barnes who lived next door put it in her big chest freezer.

It was three o'clock. Time for guests to arrive. Fiona put on a red paper hat. She made Max put on a blue one. Fiona worried about her son. The boy had begged for a party but now he did not seem very excited. He sat looking at her from under his uneven fringe. His eyes were a glossy brown. Fiona saw Dave in those eyes.

'It will be fun!' she told him. She hoped that she was right.

Fiona stood by the door waiting. The minutes passed. Still no guests. Odd. When Fiona took Max to parties they were always on time. She looked at the clock. It was twenty past three. Max had taken his hat off and was sitting on a kitchen chair. A balloon floated above him.

'Chocolate rice crispy cake?'

'Thank you.' Max ate it without any obvious pleasure.

More time passed. Fiona was no longer nervous, she was angry. How dare these people be so late? She ate a sandwich and then another.

Finally, at nearly four, there was a knock at the door.

'Oh Max! Here they are. I told you they would come.'

She rushed to the door and threw it open.

It was Mrs Barnes from next door holding the ice cream cake.

'Are you ready for this?' she asked.

Fiona didn't know what to say. The thought of trying to explain brought tears to her eyes.

'What is it?' Mrs Barnes wanted to know.

Fiona explained the problem.

'Did you put the right date on the invites?'

Fiona knew she had. 'Yes, I'm sure.'

Mrs Barnes looked at Max. 'How is he?'

'He is such a good boy. Max, do you want some cake? Come in Mrs Barnes, have a slice of cake.'

'I can't. I'm so sorry. My daughter is collecting me to visit my sister.'

Fiona took the cake.

'Not to worry,' she called and watched Mrs Barnes walk away. She didn't want to turn around and see Max sitting alone at the table.

Six o'clock. The sandwiches had begun to curl. The cake had melted. Max sat stony faced. Fiona bent down and gave him a tight hug.

131

'I am so so sorry. I do not know what happened.' In her mind she did. She cursed the snobs at the school. Spoilt brat children not willing to go to a party without a clown or goodie bag. Max was a seven-year-old. How could they be so cruel?

Fiona began to tidy up. What to do with the balloons? It seemed too violent to burst them, but too sad to leave them up.

'Would you like them in your room, Max?'

'Yes please.'

Fiona untied each balloon and then Max squeezed them up the narrow stairs to his bedroom. She watched his little legs disappear under the rainbow cloud of balloons. She wiped away her tears. Fiona put the food in Tupperware and the liquid cake remains in the bin. She got a brush and was sweeping the floor as if there had actually been a party. She moved the chairs and picked up Max's schoolbag. It seemed thicker than usual. She leaned the brush against the table. Fiona opened the schoolbag.

Inside the bag were fourteen invitations.

Never sent. Never seen.

Against the Stars

Nuala O'Connor

Ma cannot remember what time I was born. She remembers that she chose to go to the posh hospital to have me. And she remembers that my birth was the hardest of all. But she has no idea what time I came into the world.

'You must know whether it was morning or night,' I say.

'I know I screamed with pain and they gave me nothing for it,' Ma replies.

I am only asking Ma for my birth time because someone has offered to 'do my chart'. I do not actually understand what that means. I just know it has something to do with astrology, which seems glamorous and mysterious. I am a teenager and I long for both glamour and mystery. My Dublin homeplace is short on both.

'Please, Ma,' I whine, 'try to remember what time I was born.'

'Go and ask your da,' she says. 'He remembers everything.'

But I cannot ask my Da because he is against the stars. In our house we are not allowed to read horoscopes or discuss birth signs or astrology. And, according to Da, God is with him on this. God is against the stars too.

* * *

I am a Capricorn. The symbol for a Capricorn is a goat with a fish tail. I am half goat and half fish. I am a sea-goat. I like this. The astrologers tell me that, as a Capricorn, I am a determined person. I climb hills slowly and steadily. I get to the top eventually, but it takes time. My horoscope says I am an earth sign. That means that I am practical, ambitious, and that I rely on myself. All of this is true! Why, I wonder, are God, and my da, against the stars when the stars clearly speak the truth? Anyway, because I cannot tell Da why I need my time of birth, I do not ask him for it. And so my chart is not done. And that is that.

* * *

Nowadays, as an adult, I only read my horoscope by accident. But my friend tells me she rips open a fashion magazine every Sunday to see what the astrologer has to say about the week ahead. Another friend sings the praises of an online horoscope site.

'It is weirdly accurate,' she tells me. 'Try it. You will see!'

I am fascinated so I make a decision. Every day, for one week, I will read what my horoscope predicts for me and see how it compares to my real life. It cannot hurt to sneak a look, can it? So, today I go online to consult Stella von Crystal and begin my week with the stars.

* * *

Friday: 'There will be sudden changes.'
I wait for the changes all day, but nothing happens. We are in lockdown to protect ourselves from the Coronavirus and things stay the same most days. Maybe the virus means sudden changes cannot happen, I think. Maybe the virus blocks them. But, I am full of hope. Tomorrow Stella von Crystal's horoscope will surely be clearer and more accurate. It will tell me all the exciting things that are coming my way. I cannot wait!

Saturday: 'You get what you were hoping for.'

Oh goody, Stella! I am hoping to win the lottery.

I do not win the lottery.

Sunday: 'If ever there was a time to be patient, it is now.'

No kidding, Stella. The world is built on patience at the moment. We are all biding our time, being good, safeguarding our health. I am not a patient person, but I am working on it. Thanks for the reminder, though!

Monday: 'You are determined by nature.'

I am determined, Stella, that is true. I like hard work and I aim towards things and try to achieve them. But this week, Stella dear, I am mostly determined to see if you can predict my future. Wow me with your starry goods!

Tuesday: 'Amazing offers come from out of the blue.'

Amazing offers! Oh, what will they be – money? Fame? Fortune? I am *very* excited. Thanks for the good news, Stella, you have brightened up a grey morning in lockdown.

I wait all day for the amazing offers. They do not come out of the blue or out of any other place. I think you are exaggerating, Stella. Maybe you are being vague on purpose to keep me hooked. Or is it possible that you are lying to me, Stella?

Wednesday: 'Even the most determined of Capricorns needs to take a break.'

What does that mean? Can you be more specific, Stella? What am I taking a break from? The lockdown? Our days are very samey here. We get up, we work, we home-school, we walk, we eat, we sleep. Maybe I need to take a break from you, Stella. Maybe that is the break this Capricorn needs. (Can you tell that I am a little annoyed?)

Thursday: 'You owe it to yourself to wait and watch.'

Wait and watch? Wait for what? Watch what? We are back to patience again, Stella, and I have already told you that I am not good at that. And I am not getting the insights I wanted from you. (Where are my 'amazing offers', by the way? I am still waiting for them.)

Watch your step, lady. I am on to you.

Friday: 'Deal with problems now, while you can.'

Stella, to be fair, I now think that *you*, and you alone, are my problem and the time has come to deal with you, for sure. So goodbye, Stella von Crystal, goodbye. May we never cross paths again.

And then I see it. A tiny note at the bottom of the page on Stella's website. A sentence that I have never noticed before that says: 'All services are for entertainment only.'

Oh Stella, you have been wilfully wasting my time. I am not wiser about my future and I am certainly not entertained. You have fooled with me all week, my silly, starry friend. And I know, now, that it doesn't matter what time I was born, because no one will ever be doing my chart. After my week-long astrology experiment, I have come to just one conclusion. The future is not ours to own. There is only now. And, Stella, I am here to tell you that like my da – and like God – I too am against the stars.

If I Can't Have You

Roisín O'Donnell

My dad was from Galway. When I was ten, he gave me a chess set. My mum was Russian. She taught me how to play. 'Ava, you are super!' she told me. I loved playing chess. I taught my best friend Mír. His parents were Nigerian, but he was Irish. Like me.

* * *

The summer I turned eighteen, I was at my cousin's house party. It was 5 a.m. The sun was up already. The last dancers swayed in the living room, under looping fairy lights. I had flirted with Mír all night. Finally I was alone with him in the garden, playing chess. We sat on the garden wall, frowning at the chess board in the blue dawn light. Bird song fluttered in the trees above our heads. Laughter

139

floated from the house. After a long time, Mír made his move. A stupid move.

'Ha! Easy!' I shouted. I took his queen.

'Not fair, Ava!' Mír said. 'You always win!'

He kissed my bare shoulder. I fixed the strap of my purple sundress.

We walked home together, through the empty streets of Ongar. I played music on my phone and danced. 'You eejit, Ava,' Mír laughed. But I could tell by his eyes how he wanted me. It was going to happen. Only a matter of time.

* * *

I did not know someone was watching.

A quiet girl in our history class. She had watched us flirt. She had been following me on days I walked home alone, when I had football practice.

One day she stopped me at the roundabout.

'Janet is my name.'

'OK,' I said. 'Are you in my class?'

She gave a strange smile. 'Do you love him?' she asked.

'What? No!' I said, 'Sure we are only friends.'

Too late. I should have pretended I did not know who she was talking about.

140

'He is not for you,' she said.

This conversation was getting creepy.

'Right,' I said, 'I better go home.'

But my feet could not move. My soles were stuck. Janet was still smiling at me, her lips twitching. Her eyes were a weird cat-like green. A dark fringe hid her face.

'Give me your hand, Ava,' she said.

I did not want to. But my hand lifted by itself.

At her touch, I felt like I had been burnt. My hand shrunk. Then my whole body shrunk and shrunk. I tried to shout. But my voice was trapped in my mouth. Darkness came down. The world became smaller. I was trapped in a tight, dark place. I could not move.

* * *

How long was I in there? I heard the noise of the evening traffic. Waves of sound as cars and buses swished past. I heard the night sounds. Sirens, taxis, the NiteLink. All I could do was shuffle. After a while I gave up even trying to shout.

Days and nights repeated, until one morning something felt looser. I was able to move a little. I reached the tight thing that was wrapping me. I chewed a small hole. Daylight blasted in. It hurt my eyes. I kept chewing until I could push my way out.

I opened my wings.

* * *

I flew home. I landed on the kitchen window. Had they forgotten me?

It turned out I had been in the cocoon for a year or more. My little brother had grown a head taller. My mam and dad were sitting at the table. Both had tears in their eyes.

Mam turned and looked right at me. 'Oh look,' she said, 'a butterfly.'

Livid, I flew to Mír's house, across the street. He was in his bedroom with the blinds closed.

I felt hot and trapped. Wings fast, I flew.

* * *

I was a butterfly for seven summers. Seven springs of blossoms falling from the trees like pink snow. Seven winters when I hid behind spiky holly leaves.

Until the summer day I landed, tired, in a woman's long wavy hair. She was crying. Tears slid into her hair and wet my wings. I felt her broken

142

heart. She longed for a child. Slowly I melted. I felt myself dissolve. Into her skin. Into her blood. I was in the dark cocoon of her womb. I could feel her heartbeat.

* * *

I was reborn.

My memories from my new life start around the age of three. I remember a pink scooter.

A black and white dog.

Fireworks.

A blue school uniform.

Memories from my old life mixed with memories from my new. At times I remembered places I had never been. A bedroom with a unicorn poster. A mum with gentle hands. Sometimes I remembered having wings.

As I got older, I had dreams of a young man's face. A man I had never met. And I knew his name: Mír.

* * *

On the day I turned eighteen, I went to find him. I followed my feet. My body remembered where he lived, off the Ongar roundabout. I carried a chess board under my arm.

I arrived in the middle of Mír's daughter's party. Mír was sitting in the wreck of his garden, amid balloons, streamers, a half-eaten cake. Children chased each other. Parents and neighbours stood around the garden drinking. Mír held an empty beer bottle. His hair was grey.

'Hi,' I said, 'I'm a new neighbour. My name is Ava.'

He looked up quickly to check my face. He looked away. 'I knew a girl with that name once.'

By now Mír was 43 and divorced. He was living in his old childhood home. Desire had disappeared like a night-moth. Vanished. But I wanted his friendship. I wanted him to recognise me. So I placed the chess board on the table. 'I have not played in years,' Mír said.

We began to play. We studied the chess pieces as the evening sky turned deeper blue. Fairy lights hung in the trees. I had not seen him for twenty-five years. In those years, Mír had learnt very little. He made a stupid move.

I took his queen.

Man of the Match

Sheila O'Flanagan

I go to a football match nearly every week. I do not really like football but I know a lot about it. I know that Mo Salah is the best striker Liverpool has ever had. I know that VAR is ruining the game. And even though I am a woman, I know all about the offside rule.

I know about it because of Jamie. And because of Owen. But mostly Jamie. He is a Liverpool supporter. He loves Mo Salah. He made it clear to me that Mo was on nodding terms with God. He told me exactly why. He explained it very carefully so that I could be in no doubt. I nodded wisely and agreed with him about Mo. But I disagreed about VAR. I do not want to be the person who agrees with Jamie about everything. Even though I stand on the sidelines and shout 'come on, Rovers' every Saturday morning.

Rovers is the local football team. They are doing well in the league this year. So supporting them is more exciting than usual. But my heart sinks when they play in the rain. Their kit is white shorts and a red jersey. It takes forever to get the mud and grass stains out of them. I do not know why football clubs have anything white in their kit. I go mad every time I put Jamie's shorts in the washing machine. He never asks me to wash them. He just expects it.

Before I supported Rovers, I supported Wanderers. That was because I was going out with Owen back then. Owen was one of their defenders. The Wanderers players had a lot of passion for the game. This passion meant lethal tackles near the goal and, sometimes, punch-ups on the pitch.

Owen did not get into too many punch-ups but once he ended up with a black eye. He had yelled strings of insults at one of the opposition. The other guy did not take kindly to it. He belted Owen in the face. Owen's eye looked awful afterwards and I was fuming. It was my birthday. We were supposed to be going out for dinner that night. We had booked a very posh restaurant. Black eyes and posh restaurants do not go well together.

Owen and I split up shortly after that. To be honest, it was a relief. I was tired of taking second place to a soccer game. It might have been different if I was the girlfriend of a famous footballer. There is money and glamour in that. But there was no glamour in being the girlfriend of a Wanderers player and washing his dirty gear. So I was happy to stop supporting them. It was more fun to spend rainy Saturdays in the shops instead.

None of the boyfriends I had after Owen were footballers. Most liked watching matches on TV, but none of them played. The funny thing is, I liked watching too. And my boyfriends were all surprised that I knew the offside rule. They were surprised that I knew all the rules. So was I. I did not realise I had learned so much on the sidelines.

Then I met Davey and I married him. He is not a football fan. He calls all footballers eejits who would not know a day's hard work if it wandered up and kicked them in the behind. I laugh when Davey says that. I remind him that his own work is not very hard. Not physically hard anyway. Davey is a manager in a software design company. He never has to lift anything heavier than a microchip. I explained the offside rule to him once but it went over his head. Davey plays a bit of golf. He says he has to because his boss likes golf. So everyone in the company has to like it too. I've learned about golf in the ten years I've been married to Davey. But guess what? I prefer football.

Now I go to matches again on Saturdays. On my own. Without Davey. I go because of Jamie. Because I love Jamie. He is the star player on the Rovers team. When he runs out onto the pitch my heart starts beating faster. He is the best looking of them all by a mile. He is tall and sturdy. He carries himself with confidence. Every time I see him I catch my breath. Every time he scores a goal I jump up and down with excitement. I do not care who sees me.

I am not the only one who thinks Jamie is wonderful. Millie does too. She stands beside me. She comments on his play. So does her friend, Jess. I think Jess is in love with Jamie. But she is wasting her time. Because Jamie only has eyes for me. It is me he looks to when he scores. It is me he kisses after the game.

Jamie loves me as much as I love him.

I know it will not always be like this. I know I have to accept it. One day he will find another woman to kiss after his match. One day he will go home with her afterwards. One day he might give up football altogether. One day something else will be more important than scoring goals for Rovers.

But today is not that day. Today he has scored the winning goal. And now he is coming towards me, his bright smile lighting up my life.

'Did you see it?' he asks. 'Did you see it going in?'

'Of course I did.' I hug him, even though he is covered in mud. I kiss him too. 'You were brilliant.'

'Not brilliant.' He shakes his head. 'I should have scored two.'

'Next time.'

He nods. 'Next time.'

Next time will be next Saturday. Rovers are playing away. I'll have to drive Jamie to his match. The local under-tens do not have a team bus. They only have mums and dads to bring them to their matches.

But I do not mind.

I would do anything for my little boy.

My man of the match.

The Life Changing
Magic of Murder

Colm O'Regan

United45 messages me straight after it happens. He is angry.

'That man just took away my ten years' clean record, Podsy,' He says.

I reply and say, 'Yes it is terrible.' I tell him, 'He is an awful shite hawk.' We are talking about Mickman40. He is another user on the Market Town second-hand app. I am not surprised. He's a Whiner.

I had a few near misses with Mickman40 a while back. It was because of an old LA Raiders American jacket. I had it in the attic for ages. I was selling for a fiver. I sent it to him and Mickman40 said, 'This does not look like the photo on the website.'

For feck's sake. It was only a fiver. But I gave him back a euro, to keep him sweet. I was getting near to having 100 Green Thumbs then. I laugh now when I think how I was so concerned about losing my clean record. Because I am a lot more concerned now.

So now United45 has lost his clean record on Market Town. Yesterday he had the highest number of Green Thumbs on the website. More than two thousand! Today there is that one red mark next to his name. He is thinking of starting under a new account. Starting from 0. I know how he feels. The more green thumbs you have for positive feedback, the more it stings when you get the first red one. You get obsessed.

'You could appeal,' I say to him. Market Town allows you five chances to appeal any Red Thumbs.

'I am out of appeals. And Mickman40 knew that too. I offered to take it back and cancel the whole deal. It was only a hairdryer. It was working fine when I gave it to him.'

United45 has made the classic mistake. He tried to sell an electrical to a Whiner. The Whiners will always hang you on an electrical item. They take fuses out of plugs or put a little cut in a cable so that they can say the product has a fault. Just to get their money back. Just to ruin you.

COLM O'REGAN

'You are the last man standing now, Podsy,' he says to me in his last message. 'They will get you. The Whiners bring everyone down in the end.'

They won't get me though. But I don't tell him that. Because I fix it my own way. I want to keep my 100% record on the Market Town site. 1908 happy customers. That means 1908 bits of shite that I have bought or sold or swapped. I've made money off it. I get the free public transport after the accident, so sometimes I have to meet them at the bus stop or the train station. But still, not one person has ever given me the Red Thumb.

OK they have. But then they took the Red Thumb back. Even though they did not know they had.

My ex said after the accident I did not seem to care about anyone. But I cared about my clean record. And I do something about it. The whole thing started when I had 200 positive feedbacks. I was collecting a figurine. A jumping salmon. I thought I might sell it on. You could not imagine the shite that people will pay good money for. And the treasure people will let go for nothing.

The day I was supposed to deliver, the alert popped up in my email: LiverpoolFan has left negative feedback for you.

152

Negative? That was bullshit. I had told him I would be around to collect the salmon but my bus didn't turn up and my phone died. He was annoyed. He was ringing me for ages he said. I asked him to reschedule. No dice. I asked them to retract it. No reply. I was in despair. And him by pure chance I got an email. It was a newsletter from Cybercrime Monthly. I am still signed up to get it. It is just to keep in touch with my old job. I can't do that job any more.

The email was about a scam called SIM Swapping. You get the phone company to transfer some other fella's phone over to you. Without them even knowing. If I could get into LiverpoolFan's phone I could delete the red thumb myself. I had nothing to lose. It was a bit of fun really. I bought a SIM card. I had his number. I rang his phone company pretending to be him. I said my phone and SIM were shagged. Could they transfer the number over to another SIM? I knew which phone company because before we fell out, he was giving out about bad coverage.

They said 'Grand so. But we have a few security questions. What is your address?'

I knew that.

'What is your mother's maiden name? Date of birth?'

I had that from Facebook. The clown.

They said 'What was your first car?' Would you believe he had told me that as well? He said he had never had as nice a car as the Toyota Carina E since. Three out of three. So they moved his whole phone to the SIM card I'd bought. I put the card into my phone. I turned it on. There was his Liverpool Crest on the front of it. And there was the Market Town app and there was the Red Thumb against my name. Until it was not there anymore.

Because I deleted it.

I have done it four times since. Every time I sell something now, I have a great old message chat with the eejit in case I need to answer a question about them later. You would not believe what people give away about themselves. I have answered security questions like, what was the name of their first pet? (It was Flumper.)

Yes you might say that I am breaking the law. But I am just protecting my good name. Well, not my actual name. My MarketTown.com name. My good name is all I have. I don't remember much of myself before the accident.

But the latest security question I was trying to guess the answer to was: 'What was the name of your best friend in school?' I did not have a clue.

The phone company must be tightening up on the questions.

I guessed John.

'Wrong,' they said.

Daniel?

'Wrong again. I'm sorry sir,' says the lady. 'You will need to provide more "credentials."' I tell her I will be grand.

So that is why I'm in the house of a Market Town user called BillyBoots. Deleting a red thumb on Market Town on his computer.

And he does not even know I've done it. I doubt he will care. He looks in a bad way.

Make that 1909 Green Thumbs.

Cutting Grass
Paul Perry

One summer's day, my friend Mark and I were bored. We were in his house watching TV, when his mum came in and told us to turn the TV off and do something.

Mark said, 'We are doing something.'

His mum said, 'Something else.'

Mark looked at me. 'Let's make pancakes,' he said.

I did not know how to make pancakes, I told Mark. He said, 'Follow me.' So I did.

In the kitchen, he cracked eggs, and threw flour into a bowl. 'It's easy,' he said. 'I make pancakes all the time.'

We made a proper mess.

Then he put the pan on the stove, and poured the mixture in. It stuck. I smelled burning. Then I saw flames.

Mark's mum ran into the kitchen and told us to get out from under her feet.

'You could have burned the house down,' she said.

We stood outside.

'It is not even a house,' Mark said to me.

He was right. Mark lived in a flat. His dad lived in Canada. And he had never met him.

'What will we do now?' I said.

Mark pointed to the shed.

We took out the lawn mower and Mark said, 'Let's cut people's grass.'

I had once been a paper boy. Maybe that was the year before. I think it was the *Evening Press* that I delivered. It had a purple top. That paper does not exist anymore, but the memory does. The paper round did not go very well. I may have been the world's worst paper boy. I remember the strap of my bag getting caught in the chain of my bike, and being chased by a dog. I remember getting lost. The whole thing took hours. I am sure some people did not even get their papers. Sometimes, I did not get home until dark.

Mark lived near Windy Arbour, and we wheeled his mum's lawnmower all over there and around Dundrum and Sandyford.

Back then, there was a sweet shop on the corner of Bird Avenue. It was run by Mrs Fox. All the sweets were in plastic jars on a counter. She didn't sell anything else. Only sweets.

We loved Mrs Fox. And she loved us.

We rang one doorbell after another. Most people said, 'No thanks.' But a lot of people said, 'Hello, come on through and take a look.'

We pulled the lawnmower through to each back garden. And we looked at the grass. I can't say we had much experience. I can not even say we knew what we were doing at all. But we did like Mrs Fox's sweets. And that was enough of a spur.

One man wanted to show us his collection of stamps before we cut his grass. Another house was full of 'young professionals'. Mark and I stood in the grass in their garden and started to laugh.

'Are you there?'

'Where are you?'

'Can you see me?'

The grass was so long that it covered our heads. We took the job, but after a few hours we gave up. I'm not sure we even told the 'young professionals' that we had had enough. For all I know, they think we are still lost in their long grass.

At another house, on Milltown Road, we must have spent three hours cutting the grass.

'Are the blades on this thing sharp at all?' I said.

Mark turned the old lawnmower upside down. He slid his finger along a blade. He brought it back to his tongue. I'm not sure why tasting the blade was going to help him figure out if it was sharp or not.

He shook his head.

'Not the sharpest, no,' he said.

The lady who owned the house was a widow. She wanted everything neat and tidy. Mark and I wondered how much she was going to pay us. We had spent longer in her garden than anywhere else.

When she gave us half of what we thought she might, we didn't know what to say. Mark held the coin in his hands and we said thank you.

When we walked around the corner, we laughed.

We went to Mrs Fox's.

'You two have been busy,' she said.

We told her what we had been doing. She asked us to cut her grass and we did. And instead of giving us money, she gave us sweets.

We must have looked a funny pair as we leaned against the wall covered in grass cuttings.

The lawn mower stood between us as we sucked on bonbons, and cat's eyes.

That September, Mark moved school. I guess it was because he had been bullied in our school. Not the kind of bullying that looks like a black eye. A different kind of bullying. Sticks and stones, our teachers had told us, will break our bones, but words will never hurt you.

That wasn't true.

Mark knew that and so did I.

His mother had talked to the headmaster, but the bullying had not stopped.

I wish he had told me he was moving school, but he didn't. Maybe he never got the chance.

Then, one day, I was cycling to school, and I passed Mrs Fox's. But it was all locked up. Someone was painting over the sign that said Mrs Fox's.

I wanted to tell Mark, but when I called to his flat, he was never there.

It felt like things were changing very fast. I had turned thirteen that summer. And I had started to wear glasses.

I called over to Mark a few more times, but he was never there. Sometimes, a man answered the door, but I was pretty sure it was not Mark's dad.

When I said, 'Where is Mark?' the man laughed and closed the door.

I never called after that.

One day, a few years later, I heard that Mark had been hit by a car. He was crossing the road to his new school. The car had killed him.

I went to the funeral. His mother gave me a hug outside the church.

'You two,' she said. 'You two.'

I cycled past where Mrs Fox's had been on my way home. And I stopped. Through the tears, I could see us once again, as we leaned against the wall. Our hands covered in the green stain of cut grass. The pink powder of bonbons on our lips.

Amore

Deirdre Purcell

She was one of those little Dublin women you
would see bustling around the stalls in Moore
Street. She was always well turned out. In summer
she would wear a nice blouse, slacks and Clark's
sandals. In winter, warm stockings, stout shoes and
her 'good' wool coat. Her grey hair was permed
and tidy but seen only in wisps. Winter and
summer, when outdoors, Agnes wore a headscarf
tied under the chin. Like the Queen.

On this warm Saturday in June, she stopped to
smell the lilies on the flower stall but decided not to
buy. Lilies were for funerals and at her age, fifty-six,
she was already seeing too many of them.

Further on, the air was filled with the warm stink
of fish, Irish tomatoes, strawberries from Wexford
and bananas. The street rang with banter as

stallholders and customers did deals. Outside Caffrey's Butchers, a man plucked on a banjo with only three strings and iffy tuning.

'Good man, Jimmy.' Agnes fished a three-penny bit out of her purse and dropped it into the cap at his feet. 'How are things?'

'Thanks, Agnes.' He stooped to pick up the coin. 'Same-o, same-o!' They knew each other, both being early morning Mass-goers.

'You mind yourself.' She shook out her string bag. 'I have a list as long as me arm this morning.'

Less than an hour later, in her Harcourt Street flat, she had a quick dinner. Boiled egg, tea and toast. Before she set off again, she checked her handbag to make sure she had everything for the afternoon. Book, bookmark, comb, hanky, purse, Miraculous Medal, keys, her little bottle of 4711.

As he was every Saturday at two o'clock, Linus was waiting for her in the lobby of the church. He was wearing a shirt and slacks. Behind him, the doors to its dim insides were open. Light seeped colour through stained glass windows onto the banks of little candles fluttering in the breeze.

She caught the scent of incense. There must have been a funeral.

She was panting a few minutes later when they got to the foot of the Ha'penny Bridge and were climbing its slope. Linus was tall and despite being a little too fond of his food, still a fast walker. 'That diet is doing you good,' she puffed.

'Mmm!' he changed the subject. 'Did you bring your copy of the book? Ooh! Look! A Guinness barge! He leaned over the railing. Behind his back, she smiled at the sight of his tonsure, his bare pink scalp, glowing under the sun.

They had never touched except by accident or when it was absolutely necessary. Not even with a chaste hug. Both stayed inside the line of his vow of chastity.

Still hanging over the railing, he was now waving at the men on the barge who were waving back. He might have a string of degrees, she thought, but still had a childish interest in everything around him. Even the stately progress of Guinness barges.

Even her.

She often wondered why he had chosen to be friends with a woman who had left school at sixteen for a course in shorthand and typing. She had taken the first job offered – a shorthand typist for an insurance company. She had the fastest speeds in the pool and was proud of it.

164

She stayed because her skills were valued. She was paid well. By living a simple, cheap life, she could afford to take classes in Italian, French and Spanish. She could speak all three languages nearly as well as he did.

And since another of his vows was poverty, she could afford to take them all over Europe together.Over the years, they'd been to Paris a few times, to Florence, the Amalfi Coast, London and Madrid.

Once they went together to one of the oldest universities in Germany, Leipzig, where he had been invited to speak at an international seminar. The university had paid for him along with 'a guest'. He was charmed that, for once, he had been the one to issue the invitation.

At first, she had hesitated, unsure about how their companionship would be seen. Up to the last minute she had been nervous.

Once there, however, she found that nobody batted an eyelid at her presence. She even heard herself referred to as 'The speaker's lady friend'.

He laughed about this when she told him, weeks later. 'For goodness' sake, Agnes! That is what you are! You are a lady. And you are my friend. Whoever said that was only being accurate.'

165

The highlight of their travels had been when he had managed to get them into the front row of a small private audience held by Pope Pius the Tenth in the Vatican.

They were only a few feet away from him at the event and even had several minutes of face-to-face conversation with him, in Italian.

Afterwards, the pope happily agreed to a photograph. Framed in silver and hanging on the wall opposite the end of her bed in the flat, it became Agnes's most precious possession. It is the first thing she sees when she wakes every morning. She all in black with a mantilla. Linus in the robes of the Order. Pius smiling between them in his dazzling white cassock and shoulder cape.

She and Linus had met at a charity book stall he was running for his Order. She was an avid reader. The second-hand stalls along the Quays or outside Greene's bookshop kept loneliness at bay.

At his stall that day, trade was slow. Linus was on his own. When he noticed her dawdling over his volumes, he was eager to help her with selections. 'What about some of the magazines?' He pointed to a little stack of *Life*, a set of *National Geographic.* 'These were hardly touched, maybe never opened! Or here are a few *Time* magazines.

'Or,' he chuckled, 'could I interest you in a few back issues of the sizzling *Capuchin Annual*?'

She laughed along then, shyly, and asked if she could fetch him a cup of tea from another stall.

He declined, but then offered to accompany her to Bewley's some day. 'Coffee is my drink of choice and I can always do with company.'

That had been the start of it. But over the years, a routine for these Saturday afternoons had developed. Both read the same book during the week and on the Saturday, discussed it over high tea in The Capitol restaurant.

This week's book was *Rebecca*. That day, the picture showing was *All About Eve* and they made it to their seats just in time for the newsreels and trailers. Linus loved trailers, the booming music, and the deep chocolate tones of the voiceover announcing 'Coming Attractions'.

Afterwards, in the restaurant, it was clear that he had loved the picture. 'That script, that acting. Well done, Agnes, great choice! A mixed grill for me, I think?'

She had ordered oxtail soup and a salad. His piled-up grill fully hid his plate. Within minutes they were happily in discussions about *Rebecca*.

Her salad plate was clean, but he was happily demolishing his grill, when she opened the book where she had bookmarked it. 'I want you to hear this, Linus. Listen with an open mind, all right?' She began to read aloud.

But his face was twisted and as he struggled to speak, all that was coming out were soft grunts. One side of his mouth was gaping downwards and drooling heavily. He was sliding sideways off the chair.

'Linus!' She jumped up and ran over to him, putting her arms around him to stop his slide. But she couldn't support him. As she tried to hold him, she stumbled backwards.

'Stand back, please! Everyone! Call an ambulance.' A man who announced he was a doctor took charge.

As Agnes, horrified, watched this doctor's efforts, the noise of the ambulance arriving outside caused everyone to back off. Before she could be stopped, she ran to kneel beside her friend and leaned over, kissing his slack, wet mouth. Hard. Tasting. Feeling. Inhaling. Recording first kiss, last kiss, a memory for the abyss.

As she clung to him, she thought he was trying to say something on his fading breath. She used every bit of energy in her body to understand. *'Ammmmm … ammmm … o ……'* he exhaled and then it stopped.

She did not resist when the ambulance men gently lifted her and set her on a nearby chair before turning to work on him. 'You can come in the ambulance with him. You his missus?'

'No, that's all right. No ambulance.' She fished his copy of *Rebecca* from where it had lodged under the table. Holding it to her heart, she walked quietly to the door of the restaurant.

A waiter caught her when she was half way to the outer door, returning her handbag and her own *Rebecca*. She took the bag but handed back the book. 'You take this. I'll keep this one.'

Outside, she felt numb in body and mind. She stopped in the middle of O'Connell Bridge to watch another Guinness barge entering the shade under her feet. She felt the throb of its engines through the concrete footpath. Upriver, the Ha'penny Bridge was crowded with Dubliners going about their business.

For a minute or so, she stared at the spreading white fan of the barge's wake. Only then, she knew what he had been trying to say. *Amore.* The Italian for 'Love'.

She turned away from the Liffey and set out to face the empty flat in Harcourt Street.

First kiss. Last kiss.

She had no one to tell.

The Cottage
Donal Ryan

My name is Jack Ward. I'm eighty years old. I think I am anyway. My mother had so many children she lost track of the dates we were all born. My brothers and sisters are all gone now. I bought this house and bit of land fifty years ago. I've lived here on my own ever since. I used to be happy being alone. I worked hard and had company during the day. I always slept well at night.

I retired when I was seventy. My back was gone. I don't think the builders I worked for knew how old I was. I found it hard to fill my days. I used to drive into town most days for a look around. I'd go to the library or do a bit of shopping. Some days I would have a drink in Rocky O'Sullivan's. Just one, or maybe two.

I failed the eye test a few years ago and my driving licence was taken away. I started to rely on a grand-nephew to give me lifts. He told me it would cost me twenty euros each time. He spends a lot of time in the betting office. He never seems to have much luck.

I started to hear stories on the news about burglaries. I heard about people being attacked and robbed in their own homes. I'm four miles from town here. There is no other house on this road except the empty cottage next door. I have a shotgun but I don't think I'd be able to use it on a human being. Not even if they were robbing me. I used to lie in bed thinking that I should get the bus down to Thurles to the county home. I used to pray for sleep. Sometimes I even prayed for death.

A man came here one day and asked if I'd like to sell my old cottage next door. It had been sitting there for years. His job was buying old houses and doing them up and selling them on again. I said no. He asked me for my exact reasons for saying no. I told him to mind his own business.

He told me how much he would pay for the old cottage. I told him that I was not interested. I told him I was a carpenter and if I wanted to do it up I would do it myself. He went away looking very cross. I did not care that he was cross but I was sorry he was gone. Any company is good.

171

One day I had a visit from a young man and woman. They had a child with them in a buggy. They looked like they were no more than twenty-five years old. Their names were Joe and Sarah. The child's name was Joe Junior. JJ, for short.

I told them my name. We all shook hands. The man asked me if I knew who owned the old cottage. I told them that it was mine. They asked if they could rent it from me. I told them it was in very bad condition. They said that they didn't care about that. They told me that rent in the town was so high they could not afford to live there. They both had jobs but no bank would give them a mortgage.

They looked like a lovely couple. They held hands while they stood at my door talking to me. The child smiled up at me from the buggy. They were like two children, really. I thought to myself that they were trying to make a start in life but the world seemed to be trying to stop them. They seemed to be so much in love I envied them. I was in love once, a long time ago. It did not work out.

I told them that they could not live in the old cottage. It needed too much work. They thanked me for my time and left. I looked up the road after them and I wondered where their car was. A few minutes later my grand-nephew arrived. 'Did you pass a man and woman and a baby on the road?' I asked him.

'I did,' he replied. 'I know them. They are living in town in the hotel. At the taxpayers' expense. Isn't it a great country?'

I asked him what he meant by that and he told me that the young couple were homeless. He laughed as he told me. 'They are homeless, and we are supposed to pay for them to stay in a hotel. Imagine that!'

'Who are we?' I asked my grand-nephew.

'Us hard-working people who pay taxes,' he said.

'You never paid tax in your life,' I said. 'Unless they brought back the tax on gambling?' He looked a bit hurt so I gave him his twenty euros up front. We passed the young couple with their buggy as we drove into town. They waved and smiled. 'Would you not give them a lift?' I asked my grand-nephew. But he did not answer. He was still sulking.

When I got back from town that evening I went next door and looked around the old cottage. The roof wasn't in bad condition. It needed new floors and new doors and windows. It needed to be plastered, insulated and painted.

I wondered how I had left it sitting there for so long. I wondered how I had let my life get so close to its end without ever really having lived it. I thought again about the young couple and the way they had held hands. I thought about the way their child looked up at them. And the love in the child's eyes.

The next day I rang an old friend of mine. He is younger than me but we worked together for years. I gave him a list of things I needed. He told me he would deliver them in the next few days. He was true to his word. I asked him if he was interested in some work. He said that he was. Things were very quiet. He had free time. He seemed happy. I told him I would pay him in cash. 'Lovely,' he said. 'Cash is king.'

I never trusted banks. I always kept my cash in a small safe in my shed. If robbers ever came I would just hand it over. I was glad now to have something to spend my money on. My friend told me how much the job would cost. It was more than I had expected but I counted out the cash and gave it to him.

Over the next few weeks my friend and I worked all day every day. He did all the heavy lifting. I was stiff and sore every night but I slept like a baby. It was great to be busy again and to have company every day. A few more of my old pals from the building sites came and helped us out. I paid them all in cash and they were all happy. When we were finished we had a few drinks together in the newly fitted kitchen of the cottage. I felt young again. I felt happier than I had felt in years.

My grand-nephew called down the day after the job was finished. He told me he had been worried about me because I had not rang him in weeks. 'You couldn't have been too worried,' I said, 'or you would have rang *me*.' He looked a bit hurt again so I gave him his twenty euros.

'I heard you were busy anyway,' he said. 'Doing up the old cottage. Are you going to sell it?'

'I am,' I said, and his eyes lit up. He was thinking about the money I would get for the cottage and how much extra he'd be left when I died. I don't know why he's so sure I'm going to leave him everything.

'How much will you get for it, do you think?' he asked, and he licked his lips.

'I'll get for it what I get for it,' I said.

I rang the hotel in town early the next morning. I asked to speak to the manager. 'You have a young couple staying named Joe and Sarah,' I said. 'They have a small child. Can I speak to them?' The manager said that he could not put me through to them. I decided not to argue with him. I asked him to pass on a message.

'OK,' he said, but he did not seem very happy about it.

'Tell them to come out to Jack Ward's house as soon as they can. Tell them to get a taxi and I'll pay for it.'

When Joe and Sarah and JJ arrived in the taxi they would not let me pay for it. I asked them if they wanted to take another look at the cottage. They gave me a funny look. But they walked down the path from my gate to the cottage, pushing JJ in his buggy. When they saw the cottage they were silent.

'Oh God,' Sarah said eventually. 'It is beautiful.' Joe walked around the back and then he let himself in the front door.

'It's amazing,' he said. 'It's our dream house. But why are you showing it to us?'

'Because I want you to have it,' I said. 'I have a document here from a solicitor. If you sign it you will become the owners of this cottage. You will not have to pay anything. The tax will come out of my estate when I die. So my dear grand-nephew will pay it for you. He'll have no choice.'

It took me a while to convince them to sign the document. I knew they wanted to, but they were afraid. They thought they would be taking advantage of an old man. They were scared to take so much. They didn't know how little it really was.

Eventually I said to them, 'Look. I'm here on my own. I'm afraid every night and most days. If you were living next door I would feel secure. I will be able to live out my days knowing that I have good neighbours. I'm not asking you to look after me. I am just asking you to live next door to me and to be happy. To raise your child without having to worry about rent or landlords or banks.'

Joe and Sarah and little JJ come visiting most evenings. And even when they don't I can see their lights and hear them coming and going. They seem happy and carefree. They thank me over and over again. I keep telling them that they don't have to thank me. They have done more for me than I have done for them. They don't believe that, but it's true.

My grand-nephew still calls down. He has learned a lesson about giving. It was a hard lesson for him but a good one. He's still waiting for me to die but I'll keep him waiting a few more years.

I sleep well now and my days are filled with peace.

I Have a Voice

Patricia Scanlan

'You have a voice,' she says.

'No one listens,' I say.

She has found me weeping in the courtyard. It is a small, grim outdoor area. Grey stone walls. Stony ground peppered with half-dead weeds. But you can see the sky when you look up. It is the place where smokers go. A place to try and pretend that you are not a patient. An inmate. A captive. Mad, even.

But you cannot really get away from it. Cannot escape from that blue basement that holds us, caged.

They say I am addicted to painkillers. They will not believe me when I say I am crucified with burning agony. They say I pretend my pain is worse than it is. Or even that it is all in the mind.

I took an overdose of Paracetamol. I could not stand it any longer. And that is how I ended up in here. In the basement of a big hospital. The lowest of the low.

'Demand to see a consultant,' she says. 'In other hospitals I have worked in, medical needs are always met. Tests are done. This is appalling.' She looks so upset on my behalf. It warms my heart that someone cares. She is new to the 'mausoleum'. That is what we call it. *Mau-so-le-um*. I did not know what it meant, when I came here first. It is another word for grave. We are buried alive in a grave, in this place. Dull and almost dead – like zombies.

'Everything OK?' A care attendant pulls open the creaky door.

'Fine, fine.' I say quickly. 'Just having a ciggie.' I do not want him to know I have confided in the new girl. When they have their team meetings, it will be remarked on. That I was telling my sob story to the new girl. They say I am cunning. That I will do anything to get painkillers. They listen to every conversation. Watch you every minute. There is no place to be alone.

'I have to go,' my new friend murmurs. 'I will see you next week. Keep painting. It will help.' She waves as she leaves, to teach art to locked up inmates, in another hospital across town.

I move up on the shabby, chipped wooden bench to make room for another patient who has wandered out.

'She is a nice young one,' Martha says flatly. Martha is older than me, more depressed than me. Her eyes are dead in her face. Are mine like that now, I wonder? Empty. Lifeless. She stares at a vibrant red geranium, the only thing of colour, in the court yard. The only thing truly alive in this basement mausoleum. Martha worked for years in a private hospital. Her new boss bullied her. She suffered a bad breakdown.

We all have our story.

'Rudolph will be here in a few minutes.' She inhaled deeply on her fag. She makes a face. 'They have all gone nervous in there. Ha ha!' She hates our consultant.

Rudolph is his nickname. The head of the department. He runs his kingdom with a will of iron. If we do not bow, submit, and agree that he knows best, then we are 'mad', 'depressed' or 'deranged'.

Rudolph, so called because of his remarkably shiny, red nose, is a podgy, flabby man. He has the face of a drinker. Red veined, florid, his mean little eyes stare at you from under heavy lids.

The care attendant pops his head out the door. 'You are first on the list today, Martha. Best get in and not keep Doc M. waiting.'

The staff call him Doc M.

He is not even a 'Mister' or a 'Professor,' Martha told me. 'A little fat failure,' she said bitterly. 'And he takes it out on us. Shrinks, they are a law unto themselves. They can say we are cuckoo and no one can argue.'

Martha stubs out her cigarette. I follow her in. Rudolph is making his entrance. The doors of the ward are flung open. He marches along importantly. Nurses flocking after him. He is followed by his house doctor. A skinny chap, with pimply skin.

'That young fella is only out of nappies. Tiny Sir Echo,' Martha sneers. I laugh in spite of myself. My tummy is in knots. I have to face the 'team' and argue my case.

* * *

'I want to see a *medical* doctor. I want to have tests done to find the cause of my pain.' I sit at the table across from Rudolph and his minions. 'I need medical attention, as well as —'

181

'We have discussed this *many* times.' He rolls his eyes. 'Your GP has had tests done. Nothing was found. There is *nothing* physically wrong with you—'

'I am *not* imagining my pain,' I shout. I stand up and wallop the table. I kick my chair away. 'You are not LISTENING!' I roar.

'Increase her sedation,' I hear him say as I run from the room.

* * *

'We must play the game to get out of here,' Sara, my roommate, says, the next day. She is coming down from a manic episode. 'Yes, sir, no, sir, three bags full, sir,' she declares.

I am too drugged to talk. I groan in pain. I am ovulating. The pain is always worse then. I want to vomit. It is always this way.

'They have you on more drugs,' the new art teacher says, when we meet again.

'Yes,' I mutter.

'Why?'

I tell her the whole story. Of the years of pain and sickness. Of being told it is all in my head.

'I bet you have,' she says a long word, 'endometriosis.' *En-do-met-rio-sis.* 'I have the same thing. I have had it since I was a teenager. It took ages to diagnose. I have a great consultant. You must go to her.'

'*What?*' Am I hearing right? Or is it the drugs?

'Listen, when you get out of here get your GP to send you to this lady. She writes down a name, on a drawing pad. She folds it up and gives it to me. She tells me *her* story. The same as mine. But her doctor did not give up on her.

I will play the game, I decide. Yes, sir. No, sir. Three bags full, sir.

* * *

'How are you today?' Rudolph asks. His bored, brown-eyed gaze sweeps over me.

'Much better,' I say. I even manage a smile.

'Excellent. The nurses tell me you are more responsive.'

'Yes,' I murmur.

I play the game for two more months before Rudolph decides that I can leave the mausoleum.

My sister collects me. I am free.

* * *

It is a year later. I am with my consultant. The one the art teacher recommended I go to. 'You are doing very well. You are looking very well. The treatment is working. I am pleased.' She smiles at me. 'How about you?'

'I cannot believe the difference the drugs have made. And the operation.' I say. The pain is much less. I have never felt this well.'

'Don't forget your letter,' she says. I have asked her to write one saying I have been diagnosed with a disease that has a name. A *medical* disease.

* * *

My heart thumps when I see him coming. He does not even look at me. He swipes his card through the lock.

'Excuse me,' I say.

'Yes?' He does not recognise me.

'I have two letters for you,' I say.

'Oh! Oh, speak to my secretary. I do not take letters,' he says, rudely.

'You will take these,' I say. 'One is a letter from a consultant. A professor.' I rub it in. 'Stating that I have a *medical* condition.' He looks at me, perplexed. He has still not recognised me. But then

I am not drugged up, like before. My eyes are clear. My hair is cut short. I have lost a stone. I have my wits about me. I am a different woman.

'This other letter is a copy of a letter of complaint. I have sent it to the Medical Council. It is about *you*, and your neglectful treatment of *me*.' I shove it into his hand. His jaw drops. He is shocked.

'What is this nonsense? Who *are* you?' he demands.

'My name is Magdalena Nowak,' I say.

It is the proudest moment of my life. And before I turn to leave I say.

'I have a voice!'

185

The Initiation
Melatu Uche Okorie

Jumi lifted the *george* from the bed. A gasp escaped her lips at the heaviness of the lace. She ran her finger over it. She caressed the tiny hand-sewn mirrors that showed bits of her face. Her *nnenne* came and stood behind her. She was wearing a tie-dye wrapper and top Jumi had never seen before. Her *nnenne* patted the hair comb on Jumi's hair, fondly.

'The *george* is beautiful, *Nnenne*,' Jumi said. She drew her *nnenne*'s frail body as close to her own body as the lace would allow.

'I know,' her *nnenne* replied.

'Thank you very much,' Jumi whispered into her *nnenne*'s hair before releasing her.

Jumi's *nnenne* strolled to the window and stood, gazing out of it.

'Did I ever tell you the lace was given to me by my mother on my wedding day?' she asked Jumi without turning her head.

Jumi nodded, even though her *nnenne* was not looking at her to see the nod. She knew the lace meant a lot to her. *Nnenne*'s father had been a fisherman. As a young man, he had travelled to different faraway seaports to trade with the white men. The rumour in the village then was that he was involved in the slave trade. Jumi's *nnenne* still insists those rumours were started out of jealousy because her father had become a powerful and wealthy man. He had showered *nnenne*'s mother with beautiful gifts. The *george* was one of them.

'My father gave it to my mother at my birth. She passed it on to me during my traditional wedding. As soon as the elders called for me to come out to give the groom his first drink, my mother rushed into my room. She draped this lace over me. I was led out to a loud cheer. People fell over themselves to touch the lace. They had never seen a *george* like this one before.'

Jumi's *nnenne* wiped her eyes with a fingertip. 'The mirrors gave fat reflections of people's faces. It was so funny.'

187

Jumi placed the lace back on the bed and went to take her *nnenne*'s hand.

'Your mother loved it too.' Jumi's *nnenne* continued. 'She used to sneak into my room to admire the *george* in its box. I used to tell her the *george* would be hers one day. She wanted me to give it to her during her own initiation into the womanhood ceremony. I said no. She asked for it again during her traditional wedding. Again, I refused. I wanted to give it to her at a much bigger occasion. Like at the birth of her first child, you see. I thought it would be best.'

She turned her head from the window to look at Jumi. Her eyes pleading for Jumi's understanding. 'Just the way my own father did when I was born.'

'Shh, *Nnenne*, it's OK. I understand.' Jumi said as she hugged her *nnenne* again.

'Your mother left the earth too soon ...' Jumi's *nnenne* added in a muffled voice, her head buried in Jumi's shoulder.

Jumi had been told from the time she was old enough to understand things that her mother had died minutes after giving birth to Jumi. Jumi's father, heartbroken with grief at his wife's death, had run away from the village. His body was found months later. He had drunk himself to death.

188

'I think I can hear some drumming, *nnenne*,' Jumi lied as she gently stepped away from her.

Jumi's *nnenne*'s face brightened.

'The drumming signals the start of the initiation. Quick, Jumi, we must hurry!'

Jumi's *nnenne* clapped her hands excitedly. 'Can you imagine that after today's ceremony you will officially be of age to marry? You must wear the *george* to the arena for your dance. You will surely get lots of suitors.'

'*Nnenne*, you must stop saying such things. You know that I do not want to get married now. I want to go to college and train to be a teacher.'

'But your poor *nnenne* is getting old, Jumi. Do you not want me to carry your children?'

Before Jumi could answer, a knock came at the door. It was Jumi's aunties. Stella, Ugo and Ebele. They had come to help Jumi get ready for her initiation into womanhood. They saw the *george* spread out on the bed and stooped down to admire it.

'It's the *george*,' Auntie Stella was the first to speak.

'It is so beautiful.' Auntie Ugo took the *george* from the bed. She draped it across her chest. Then she went to stand in front of the mirror.

'You will surely get good suitors tonight,' Auntie Ebele said. 'We might be back by the next market day to celebrate your wedding.'

'But I don't want to marry anyone yet!' Jumi cried. 'I want to go to college to train to be a teacher.'

Aunties Stella, Ugo and Ebele clapped their hands excitedly. 'We must hurry,' they said all at once, ignoring Jumi.

They each grabbed a tube of henna ink and began to draw tiny stars and moons on Jumi's face. Then her neck, hands and feet. They put the *george* over Jumi's head. As it flowed down, the mirrors sparkled, casting tiny lights all over the room. After that came Jumi's *nnenne*'s beads. Jumi's aunties Stella, Ugo and Ebele placed some beads round Jumi's neck. They slid some round her wrist and put some round her ankles.

When they were finished, they stepped back from Jumi and asked her to walk around. But when Jumi tried to walk, the heaviness of the *george,* and the beads made it difficult for her to move.

'I can't walk!' Jumi cried. 'I have to take some of the beads off.'

'You mustn't,' shouted Auntie Ebele.

'It will ruin the look,' Auntie Stella cried.

'Everything is just perfect!' Auntie Ugo exclaimed.

'My beautiful Jumi will find the perfect suitor today,' said Jumi's *nnenne* as they hurried Jumi out of the room.

Glossary of words:

George: A fabric, comes in different designs, used for clothing by Igbo women of Nigeria. It is said to have come from India, and was brought into Africa as a form of trade. It was named after one of the British King Georges'.

Nnenne: A term for grandmother. Nne is mother, so Nnenne is by extension, mother-mother. Can be used in the shortened form of Nene.

About the Authors

Blindboy Boatclub is one half of the Rubberbandits, as well as a comedian, musician, satirist, performance artist, writer, activist, podcaster and polymath. His story collections, *The Gospel According to Blindboy* (2017) and *Boulevard Wren and Other Stories* (2019) have been best-sellers. His weekly podcast reaches over a million listeners monthly, and his new television series with the BBC, *Blindboy Undestroys the World*, is out in 2020.

Dermot Bolger is one of Ireland's best known poets, novelists and playwrights. His most recent book from New Island Books is a collection of stories, *Secrets Never Told*. www.dermotbolger.com

Marita Conlon-McKenna is one of Ireland's best loved authors. Her award winning work includes *Under the Hawthorn Tree* (1990), *Rebel Sisters* (2016) and *The Hungry Road* (2020).

Sinéad Crowley is the author of the DS Claire Boyle series, police procedural / psychological thrillers set in Ireland. The first book in the series *Can Anybody Help Me?* was an Irish bestseller and shortlisted for Crime Book of the Year at the Irish Book Awards 2014. The sequel *Are You Watching Me?* was shortlisted for the same award in 2015 and book three *One Bad Turn* will be published in June 2020. Sinéad is also Arts and Media correspondent with RTÉ News in Dublin.

Martina Devlin has written seven novels, a short story collection, two non-fiction books and a play. She has a weekly current affairs column in the *Irish Independent* and presents a books podcast, *City of Books*, for Dublin UNESCO City of Literature.

Roddy Doyle has written more than twenty books, including twelve novels, the most recent of which is *LOVE* (2020). His novel *Paddy Clarke Ha Ha Ha* won the Booker Prize in 1993.

He co-founded the highly acclaimed Fighting Words project, and has written three Open Door novellas.

Christine Dwyer Hickey's novel *Tatty* (2004) is the Dublin One City One Book choice for 2020. Her latest novel *The Narrow Land* (2020) is winner of the Walter Scott Prize and the Dalkey Literary Award.

Rachael English is the author of five novels. *Going Back* (2013) which was shortlisted for the most-promising newcomer award at the Irish Book Awards, *Each and Every One* (2014), *The American Girl* (2017), which was a number one bestseller in Ireland, *The Night of the Party* (2018) and *The Paper Bracelet* (2020). She is also a presenter on the RTÉ radio programme, *Morning Ireland*.

Patrick Freyne is a features writer at *The Irish Times*. His debut collection of essays *OK, Let's Do Your Stupid Idea* is being published September 2020 by Sandycove.

Yan Ge is a fiction writer in both Chinese and English. She is the author of thirteen books in Chinese, including six novels. She started to write in English in 2016. Since then, her writing has been published in *The New York Times*, *TLS*, *Brick*, and elsewhere.

Carlo Gébler is a writer. He teaches at HMP Maghaberry and Hydebank College and the Oscar Wilde Centre for Irish Writing, Trinity College, Dublin. He has been a prison teacher since 1991. His latest books include *The Dead Eight* (2011), *The Innocent of Falkland Road* (2017) and *Aesop's Fables: The Cruelty of the Gods* (2019). *Tales We Tell Ourselves*, his selection of tales from *The Decameron* will be published by New Island in 2020.

Ciara Geraghty lives in Dublin. She is the author of seven novels, one Open Door novella, and many short stories. She can be found on Facebook (@CiaraGeraghtyBooks), Twitter (@ciarageraghty) and Instagram (@ciara.geraghty.books).

Ruth Gilligan is the author of five novels including, most recently, *The Butchers* (2020). She works as a Senior Lecturer in Creative Writing at the University of Birmingham and is an ambassador for the global storytelling charity Narrative 4.

Emily Hourican is an author and journalist. She has published five novels and one book of non-fiction. She writes regularly for the *Irish Independent* and the *Sunday Independent*. Born in Belfast, she grew-up in Bruxelles and lives in Dublin with her husband and three children.

Úna-Minh Kavanagh won the award for Social Activist of the Year with *U Magazine* for her initiative, 'We Are Irish' in 2017. She edits the good news website WeAreIrish.ie. Her memoir, *Anseo,* about the Irish language, identity, and racism was published in 2019. She is a blogger and live-streamer in English and in Irish.

Louise Kennedy has been published in *The Guardian*, *The Irish Times*, *The Stinging Fly* and on BBC Radio 4. Her debut short story collection, *The End of the World is a Cul de Sac*, is due Spring 2021 from Bloomsbury.

Sinéad Moriarty's novels have sold over 700,000 copies in Ireland and the UK. She has won over readers and critics by telling stories that are humane, moving and relevant to modern women. She lives in her native Dublin with her husband and their three children.

Graham Norton is a BAFTA award winning comedian, actor, TV and radio presenter. He hosts *The Eurovision Song Contest*, as well as his acclaimed TV and radio shows. A #1 bestselling and award winning author of two novels, his third, *Home Stretch* is due October 2020.

Nuala O'Connor lives in County Galway. Her forthcoming fifth novel, *NORA*, is about Nora Barnacle, wife and muse to James Joyce, and will be published in 2021. Nuala is editor at flash e-zine *Splonk*. www.nualaoconnor.com

Roisín O'Donnell won the Irish Book Award for Short Story of the Year 2018. Her debut short story collection *Wild Quiet* (2016) was shortlisted for several prizes. She is working on a novel.

Sheila O'Flanagan is the author of twenty-five #1 bestselling novels and three collections of short stories for adults. She has also written two novels for children and young adults, and a novella for

Open Door. Her work has been translated into over 20 languages.

Colm O'Regan is a columnist, broadcaster, comedian and author. He has published four books of non-fiction – the three bestselling books of Irish Mammies and *Bolloxology* – and a novel, *Ann Devine: Ready for Her Close-Up* (2019). *Ann Devine: Handle with Care* (2020) is his second novel. Originally from Cork, he now lives in Dublin with his wife Marie and daughters Ruby and Lily.

Paul Perry's most recent poetry collection is *Blindsight* (above/ground press). He co-authored four international bestsellers as Karen Perry. His novel *The Garden* is forthcoming from New Island in 2021.

Deirdre Purcell is a former Abbey Theatre actress, TV and Radio Presenter, award winning journalist, and author of critically acclaimed #1 bestselling novels, biographies, and works of non-fiction. She has written two novellas for Open Door.

Donal Ryan is a novelist and short story writer from Nenagh, Co. Tipperary. He has won several awards for his fiction and has twice been nominated for the Booker Prize. He teaches Creative Writing at the University of Limerick.

Patricia Scanlan is the #1 bestselling author of twenty novels, short story collections and works of non-fiction, which have sold millions of copies worldwide. She is the Series Editor of the award winning Open Door series of books, to which she has contributed four novellas.

Melatu Uche Okorie is a Nigerian writer based in Ireland. Her collection of short stories, *This Hostel Life*, was published in 2018 by Skein Press.

About NALA

What is NALA?

The National Adult Literacy Agency (NALA) is a charity and membership-based organisation. We work to support adults with unmet literacy and numeracy needs to take part fully in society and to have access to learning opportunities that meet their needs. NALA does this by raising awareness of the importance of literacy, doing research and sharing good practice, providing distance learning services and by lobbying for further investment to improve adult literacy, numeracy and digital skills.

What is literacy?

Literacy is an essential life skill that involves listening, speaking, reading, writing, numeracy and using everyday technology to communicate, access services and make informed choices.

Literacy also has personal, social and economic parts to it. Literacy helps people and communities to reflect on their situation, explore new possibilities and make changes.

We use different types of literacy for different things. Our skills tend to be 'spiky', which means that we can be good at one thing but have difficulties with another. Many adults who have not practised their literacy skills for a number of years can become 'rusty'. Literacy and numeracy are like muscles – if we don't use them, we lose them.

Literacy and numeracy needs in Ireland

The OECD Survey of Adult Skills (2013) found that 18% of adults (between the ages 16 and 65) find reading and understanding everyday texts difficult. This means that 521,550 adults struggle with reading a leaflet, short story, bus timetable or medicine instructions. 25% of adults (754,000 people) have difficulties using maths in everyday life, for example basic addition, working out a bill or calculating averages.

How do I improve my literacy and numeracy?

Literacy and numeracy skills are part of everyday life. Think of all the notices and signs around us, how we use money every day or send text messages. Everywhere we go, we see text, numbers and technology.

If you would like to brush up on your skills, you can do that through:

– NALA's Distance Learning Service,

or

– Attending your local adult literacy service (run in your local Education and Training Board)

NALA's Distance Learning Service

The National Adult Literacy Agency (NALA) has been offering a Distance Learning Service since 2000.

There are two ways to learn with us and you can use both.

1. Learn with a tutor on the phone

We can work with you over the telephone, through the post or on the internet.

- Everything is free.
- You decide what to study. There is no set course.

202

- We call when it suits you – you just tell us when. There is no class schedule.
- Normally we make one call per week for up to 30 minutes.
- We keep working with you until you meet your goals.
- 7 days a week, early morning to late evening.

How do I contact the service?
- Ring our Freephone support line on 1800 20 20 65 or text 'LEARN' to 50050.
- We are open Monday to Friday, from 10 a.m. to 5 p.m.

We can also give you details on your local adult literacy service.

2. Learn online

Learn with NALA is a new website that will help you improve your skills and get a qualification if you want to. See https://courses.nala.ie/ for more information.

We have eight courses at Level 2 available and Level 3 is coming soon.
1. Reading (5 credits)
2. Writing (5 credits)

3. Quantity and Number (10 credits)
4. Pattern and Relationship (5 credits)
5. Personal Decision Making (5 credits)
6. Using Technology (5 credits)
7. Setting Learning Goals (5 credits)
8. Listening and Speaking (5 credits)

ETB Adult Literacy Services

There are over 100 local adult literacy services around the country.

You can attend your local centre to work with trained tutors on a one-to-one basis or in small groups. The service is free and confidential.

You can get two to six tuition hours per week. The local Adult Literacy Organiser will meet you and find a suitable tutor for you. There are currently about 65,000 adults learning in literacy centres around the country.

For information on your nearest service, contact the NALA freephone support line on 1800 20 20 65 or check out the NALA website at www.nala.ie.

For readers of the Open Door series in the UK, continue your reading journey with The Reading Agency

The Reading Agency is here to help keep you and your family reading. If you have enjoyed this book why not take a look at our programmes:

Take part in **Reading Ahead** with your local library, college or workplace and **challenge yourself to complete six reads** to receive a certificate. **readingahead.org.uk**

Celebrate reading and books on **World Book Night** which takes place every year on 23 April. **worldbooknight.org**

Join **Reading Groups for Everyone** to find a reading group near you, set up your own group or discover new books. **readinggroups.org**

Read with your family as part of the **Summer Reading Challenge** which inspires children to read more and share the books they love.
summerreadingchallenge.org.uk

For more information on these Reading Agency programmes, please visit our website:
readingagency.org.uk

Find an **Open Door** or a **Quick Reads** book in your local bookshop or public library. Quick Reads are short books written by bestselling authors for new, lapsed and less confident readers.
www.readingagency.org.uk/quickreads

The Reading Agency is a national charity tackling life's big challenges through the proven power of reading.

THE
READING
AGENCY

www.readingagency.org.uk   @readingagency

The Reading Agency Ltd. Registered number: 3904882 (England & Wales) Registered charity number: 1085443 (England & Wales) Registered Office: Free Word Centre, 60 Farringdon Road, London, EC1R 3GA The Reading Agency is supported using public funding by Arts Council England.